# THE DEGRADATION
# OF GOLD

by John Neu

Hillside House
Townsend, Wisconsin
2021

9 781667 120669

# DEDICATION

With much gratitude to my niece, Kris Parins,
who designed and produced most of my books

# ONE

Sam Ives, sitting in the bay window of the coffee shop, looked up over his glasses and the top of the New York Times just as his wife walked by with another man, a big, blustery fellow walking partly behind her and talking over her shoulder. Alma looked straight ahead and brought one hand up to the side of her face, as if to shield either her ear or her silver hair from the tumble of words. She didn't see Sam and he leaned to the window to watch them disappear down the sidewalk crowded with students on their way to class, his last sight the broad backside of Alfred Stubblefield and, in front of him, just a glimpse of Alma's lavender dress.

"Stubblefield," he grunted, and snapped the Times to attention again. A student at the table close to him looked up to see if he had been addressed, then returned to his book. Sam's crossed legs in white seersucker were planted on the seat of the table's second chair. His white seersucker sport coat hung open on both sides of a big stomach that pressured his belt buckle and the buttons of a white shirt. Through the shirt pocket the bright colors of a cigarette pack glowed. A red necktie, with occasional burn holes from cigarette ash, hung from his stout neck, the red of the tie visible around the edge of a collar that had not been properly turned down.

Sam touched his pack of cigarettes and looked over his shoulder at the smoke-free room. A row of students in shorts and T-shirts on this early spring day glanced nervously at their wristwatches, assessing the length of the line to the counter where a lone girl behind castles of bakery attempted to manufacture a variety of coffee drinks while at the same time collecting money. All the smokers sat outside at plastic tables under two young ash trees with vandal-broken limbs.

Sam reached for a coffee mug lettered Brew Kup in red. He leaned slightly forward to keep his shaking hand from spilling the coffee. Why would she come down State Street, instead of Langdon, he thought? Serves her right, running into Stubblefield. The coffee had gotten cold. He looked at his watch and then at the sidewalk even more crowded with students now that the eight-fifty class hour was but five minutes away. He reassembled the parts of the newspaper scattered on the table top and reached under the table for the old leather briefcase that even after years in the Midwest still reminded him of the streets of Manhattan and his early days as a book scout for rare-book dealers there. He unbuckled the flap and reached inside for the book catalog that had come in the mail yesterday: an elaborate catalog of early science books with full-page colored plates of some of the more important books. These days, much to Sam's regret, most of the dealers listed their books online, avoiding the expense of printed catalogs, not to mention the colored plates. He paged through it, studying the prices.

By the time Sam had finished the catalog, the coffee shop had emptied of students, the tables outside were almost deserted, and the sidewalk was again navigable. On the campus a multitude of hallway bells had rung simultaneously and classroom doors had closed on resigned students. Sam folded the newspaper into one section of his briefcase, stuffed the book catalog into another, and pushed his heavy body up from the chair. He flexed his stiff knees, checked his wristwatch, and went out into the spring sunshine, swinging the briefcase by its worn handle.

The street that ran between the university campus and the state capitol building had been converted to a semi-mall with a narrow two-lane road squeezed by wide sidewalks on either side. Only buses and delivery trucks were allowed to enter the road. A UPS truck had parked half over the curb in front of a store selling university-logo sweatshirts and other paraphernalia. A city bus inched between the truck and a cab that had pulled onto the opposite curb. Sam held his breath as he hurried through the blue exhaust the bus pumped. At Fountain Way, an uphill passage between an apartment building and a clothing store, three workmen at different levels scrubbed the concrete bed of an imitation stream that would, when turned back on, flow down from an assembly of boulders at the top. A cluster of street people sat on one of the concrete retaining walls desperately smoking and passing a paper-bag wrapped bottle. Alongside a sleeping dog and an open guitar case seeded with a few coins, a young man in bib overalls and no shirt plucked at his guitar and sang. Sam stopped in front of the boy and dug the pack of cigarettes from his shirt pocket.

"Where you from, young man?" he asked, lighting a cigarette.

"What?" the boy said. He seemed dazed, called out from inside the song he sang.

"Are you from here?" Sam asked.

The boy said, "No. Not here."

"Did you write that song?"

The boy smiled. "Yeah. It's one of my songs."

"Nice song," Sam said. He pulled out his wallet and dropped a dollar into the boy's guitar case. "Get some breakfast," he said. "You don't look so hot."

In the next block he stopped in front of Lowell's Bookshop to study through the plate glass window the used books displayed in groups among potted plants and antique prints of fruit and birds. Nothing was old enough to interest him and he was about to turn away when he saw inside the still dark store Alice Lowell hurrying toward the window from the old desk that served as her counter. One of her plump arms was raised high, and with the other she pulled at Sam to come in. He took a last draw on his cigarette, snuffed it on the heel of his shoe, and put the butt in his coat pocket. As he walked into the alcove entryway, Alice was already unlocking the door for him.

"Sam," she said, breathless. "I'm so glad to have caught you. I'm not open yet, but I have something I want you to look at."

She was a stout woman, with graying hair as disarrayed as bunched newspaper, wire-rimmed glasses, a dandruff-flaked blue sweater over an apple green dress. Sam knew that she always suspected he bought books from her and resold them again at enormous profit, so he was surprised she would ask his opinion of anything. She seized the sleeve of his white jacket and gripped it in a tight fist to all but drag him back toward the desk.

"Good lord, Alice," Sam grunted, his briefcase dangling from the seized arm.

Since she hadn't opened yet, lights over the book stacks in the back of the shop had not been turned on. Alice dragged him between darkened book shelves sagging under the weight of hundreds of books into a small back room lined with more overflowing bookcases. Even the wooden floor of the old building seemed to sag. She released his arm, pulled a cord to switch on a ceiling light, and knelt on both knees beside two cardboard boxes that had once contained apples but now contained thick volumes in green bindings. Several of the books were piled next to one of the boxes.

"These ones are all just an old *Britannica*, but look at this," she said. She pushed herself up using the box of books as support and held out to Sam a thin quarto volume bound in heavy gray paper that had been partly creased. "It was sticking out part way from one of the volumes at the bottom. Got pressed against the side of the box, so that's why it's creased like. I think it might be valuable."

Before he could take the book, something poked Sam in the back of his thigh. "What the ... " he said, jumping aside.

"Go away, Belle," Alice said. "Go lie down on your pillow."

The old yellow lab looked up at Sam for sympathy, then turned and waddled back toward the front of the shop. Sam tugged his white pants leg around to see if it had been spotted.

"It's dated 1678," Alice said, holding open the pamphlet. She tapped the large bold type of the title page as she handed it to Sam. "It's something about gold."

Sam tucked his briefcase under one arm, pushed his glasses higher, and took the book. He studied the title page a moment.

"It's in good shape," Alice said, "for that old. Except it got wrinkled like that."

"Of a degradation of gold," Sam read. "made by an anti-elixir. A strange chemical narrative." He turned the page over and back. "It appears to be anonymous."

"1678 is pretty old," Alice said. "Right?"

"There were hundreds of these little anonymous tracts," Sam said. "Mostly political, although this one seems to be about chemistry. Alchemy, I think. Probably not worth a great deal. Especially since it's creased."

"I knew you'd say that," Alice said. She reached for the book again.

"What's this now?" Sam said. He had turned to the inside front cover to look for bookplates or signatures. "Look at that now." He faced the book to Alice, holding it open with a cigarette-stained thumb.

"What?" she said, peering at the book.

"The bookplate. Hugh Montclaire." An engraved elaborate coat of arms stood over "Hugh Montclaire" in bold capitals.

"So?"

"The Montclaire sale back in the forties was famous. A great book collection. There's a stain here, right under the Montclaire plate, looks like maybe another bookplate that's been removed."

"Well, I've paid for it." Alice pulled the volume away from Sam and clutched it to her breast as if Hugh Montclaire himself were rushing toward her, hands extended. She looked over Sam's shoulder at the sound of the front door opening. "I have to go open," she said.

"Who'd you get it from?" Sam asked.

"I'm not saying. It was stuck in that encyclopedia, which I paid for, so it's mine now."

"Alice. Whoever the owner was probably didn't know it was there."

"You don't know that." She bent to tuck the book back into the box. "I have to go up front. Someone's come in." She pushed around Sam, turning the big man in her wake, and started down the aisle toward the store front, muttering, "I knew I shouldn't have mentioned it to you."

"You really should tell the fellow you bought it from, Alice, to be fair about it," Sam said, following down the path of her unique perfume, a combination of rose dust and old paper overlaid with some new scent she must be trying. Her big hips swayed, whipping her green skirt about.

She stopped in front of the old desk cluttered with dangerously leaning towers of books and a huge old cash register. The yellow lab came out from under the desk to greet her. "Now I've lost a customer," she said, looking around. "Can I help you? Anyone here?" She took up her stance behind the desk. "Come lie down, Belle."

"What are you going to do with it, Alice?" Sam asked.

"You want to buy it?"

"Not without knowing it's really yours."

"It's mine alright. I'll find out what it's worth, too."

"Two or three hundred," Sam said. "That would be a lot for an anonymous pamphlet, creased like it is. I'd give you two-fifty for it."

"We'll see," Alice said. "I'm going to look it up first."

"Well, I'll buy the encyclopedia then," Sam said. "It's an eleventh edition. I've always wanted an eleventh *Britannica*. Is it all there? What'll you take for that?"

"I get seventy-five for an eleventh *Britannica*."

"Alright. It's not in very good shape, though. One of those sets where they bound two volumes in one.. But I'll give you seventy-five for it." Sam unbuckled the straps of his briefcase and dug out a checkbook.

"Anybody in here?" Alice hollered as Sam wrote a check. "I thought I heard someone." She took the check and inspected it.

"I could go three hundred for the pamphlet," Sam said. "At most."

"Not till I find out what it's really worth," Alice said. "I'm going to look it up."

Sam laughed and started toward the entryway. Behind him Alice called, "You're just trying to cheat me, Sam Ives. Belle, come lie down. Where are you going?" The dog, wagging its tail, lumbered toward the back of the store. It turned the corner of a row of book shelving and looked up at someone waiting there in the darkened aisle.

೧೮

Outside, Sam stepped into an increasing rush of students on the wide sidewalk. Lowell's Bookshop shared a wall with Walgreens. The drugstore, a yellow brick building with slit windows that had replaced the plate glass broken so often in the turbulent days of student demonstrations, extended to the corner of this last block of State Street where the campus began. Students oblivious to traffic crossed at all angles to reach the mall between the University Bookstore and the University Library. Sam stopped at the corner to wait for the protection of students to cross to the campus.

Food carts lined the mall like small houseboats moored to the light posts. Only the two that offered coffee and sweet rolls were open. In the brick-tiled circle between the bookstore and the library, a bald man with a white bib apron erected boxes of fruit from inside a square of folding tables while a young man washed down the surrounding bricks with a hose attached to the side of the Catholic chapel. The smell of wet bricks and concrete and remnants of yesterday's produce reminded Sam of the early morning streets of Manhattan. He touched the pack of cigarettes in his shirt pocket, tempted to sit on one of the mall benches to smoke. He glanced at his watch, sighed, and crossed to the library's revolving doors.

A young Asian woman behind the counter at the entry turnstile, her hands folded seemingly in prayer, smiled and nodded as if she knew him. Sam showed his identification and pushed through the turnstile. The computer terminals that lined the wall of the library's foyer were deserted this early in the morning. Their blank screens watched Sam walk to the bank of elevators and turn right to the single elevator that served the Department of Special Collections on the library's top floor. He pushed the call button and waited, watching above the door the row of numbered circles track with descending light the elevator's approach. With a ding, the elevator door slid open and Sam stepped into the lighted cubicle and pressed the nine button. He swung his brief case against his pants leg until the door opened again to a foyer lit by globes imbedded in the ceiling. A wide path of rubberized carpet crossed the parquet floor to tall glass doors in a glass wall behind which exhibit cases like giant cubes stood in islands of spotlight. Sam pulled open the heavy door and walked through the exhibit cases without looking at the books stretched open on their backs or on plastic stands as if in various states of torture. Through another glass door he entered the reception area where to his left a wall of card-catalog cabinets faced in challenge a wall of computer terminals. Behind a counter, Mavis Martin stood with a telephone pressed to her face. She turned her back on him as if she had been caught in something illegal. Sam plopped his briefcase noisily on the counter. He waited, hearing her whisper into the phone, until she turned, smiling and hugging the phone into her bosom to smother a voice that had continued to talk.

"Mr. Vandersteen's not in yet," she said.

"It's nine-thirty," Sam said. He looked up at the clock over Mavis's head.

"Well, he should be here shortly," Mavis said. "He called earlier. Just a minute." She turned her back and said to the phone "Two people for four nights then." She bent to jot something on a notepad, the phone at her ear lost in the downfall of long black hair. She hung up the phone and came to the counter, leaning her forearms on the marble top. "I don't know what to tell you, Mr. Ives," she said, smiling. "He called about nine. I thought he'd be here by now. He's probably having coffee somewheres." She rolled her eyes.

"He called me yesterday about an appraisal he wanted," Sam said. "You know anything about it?"

"Oh, that. There're boxes of books in the workroom. That's probably it. Professor Roth's daughter brought them in a couple weeks ago. He's the one was in the plane crash, you know."

"He left his books to the library?"

"His daughter brought them in. They want an appraisal for taxes. She called about it again yesterday. I can take you down and show you if you want." She looked over Sam's shoulder at the glass-walled reading room where several walnut tables stood empty. "There's nobody in here now anyway. I'll get the student that's shelving to sit at the desk."

"Can I bring this?" Sam said, swinging up his briefcase.

"Sure. We trust you, Mr. Ives." Mavis laughed and pushed at Sam's arm. She was taller than Sam, but thinner. Gigantic red geraniums with even bigger green leaves covered the loose blouse she wore. Sam noticed she was looking over his shoulder.

"Oh, here he comes now," she said. "Mr. Vandersteen." She hurried Sam out from behind the counter, almost pushing him. "He likes me to get permission before I take anybody downstairs," she said. "Pretend you're waiting for him."

"I am waiting for him," Sam said, annoyed.

Otto Vandersteen strolled toward them proudly self-aware. A small man, the polished top of his bald head was only slightly higher than the reception counter next to him. He pressed a leather folder to the breast of his expensive brown suit and with his free hand adjusted the knot of a yellow silk tie. He seemed annoyed at being stopped before he made the cover of his office.

"Here you are," Mavis said. "Mr. Ives has been waiting for you." She looked maliciously at the wall clock.

"Good morning, Sam," Vandersteen said. He held out an arm from which his hand hung like something to be admired rather than shaken.

Sam squeezed the hand harder than he normally would have with anyone else but regretted it when the hand seemed to collapse in his much larger one. "I'm here about the appraisal, Otto," he said. He held up his briefcase as if to prove it.

"Well, come into my office," Vandersteen said. "We'll have a chat first."

"Do you want me to show him downstairs?" Mavis said. "Those boxes."

"No, no, put the books on a book truck and have them brought up to the reading room."

"All of them?" Mavis said. "I've only got one student here."

"Well, one should be able to handle the job, don't you think, Mavis. Come along, Sam."

"This is Ted Roth's library you want me to appraise?" Sam said to Vandersteen's back while the little man attempted clumsily to unlock the door to his office.

"No, no, not the whole library," Vandersteen said. He shook the door handle and twisted the key again. He pushed the door open. "Just the rare books. The others are going to the general stacks. I've been meaning to call you about it, and now the daughter's after me." He sighed audibly as he entered the room and crossed the carpet to a large walnut desk in front of a wall of built-in bookcases. He had ignored the light switch by the door, but the room was bright with morning sunshine pouring through two large windows that looked over the roofs of the stores lining State Street. Before sitting in a tufted-leather chair, he switched on a floor lamp that leaned on a curved metal arch over his desk. He laid the leather folder carefully on the desk and sat forward in his chair with his elbows on the desk. In a Majolica jardiniere on the corner of the polished walnut, a single orchid blossom on a long stem hovered near Vandersteen like a gaudy butterfly about to land.

"Sit down, sit down, Sam," he said. He still retained, after fifty years in the United States, traces of a Dutch accent that Sam would have thought an affectation if it hadn't reminded him of the hint of German still in his own wife's speech. Even though she had been born in New York she had acquired it from a mother who had learned only what English was necessary, insisting they would return to Munich as soon as the war was over.

"I'd no idea Ted Roth had rare books," Sam said. He propped his briefcase against the leg of an armchair and shifted his butt on the hard seat, seeking the thickest flesh cushion. The chair seemed lower than most chairs and he had always suspected Vandersteen had chosen it so he himself would seem to loom behind the burnished barge of his desk.

"A small collection of science things he'd managed to pick up over the years," Vandersteen said. "Actually, some of them quite nice, I believe. He collected Robert Boyle. As he never let me forget. He was fanatic about it."

Sam began habitually to roll his red tie from its tip up over his big stomach. "Really? I'm surprised he never tried to buy anything from me." He pushed the tie flat again, brushing at cigarette burns like crumbs, and looked up. "How many books are we talking about? To appraise."

"Oh, I'd say twenty-five volumes, maybe a few more. Seventeenth-, early eighteenth-century, from what I saw. Many editions of Robert Boyle."

Sam pulled himself up in the chair. "Sounds interesting. I'd no idea. Did you get Roth's archives, too? Now that'd be something. They must be huge. He was famous. Nobel Prize and all."

"No, thank God. The Archives Department ... June, his daughter ..." Vandersteen stood and turned his back to look out the big windows, his clutched hands behind him very white against the dark brown of his suit. "I'm in a bit of a spot here, Sam." He turned back and pulled the high-backed chair to him on its casters, standing behind it as if it were a shield. "His daughter believes anything the great man as much as glanced at is something sacred to be preserved for the hoards of historians she imagines will soon be pounding on our doors. I mean, really, Sam." He sat down again and stroked the remembered hair on his shining scalp. "I realize he was well known, but ..."

"Famous, Otto," Sam said. "He was famous. Probably the most famous man this university has ever produced."

"In science, perhaps." Otto changed the direction of an antique Esterbrook pen lying on its reflection. He glanced at the three slim volumes of his own self-published poetry clutched between antique trefoils placed carefully a foot from the orchid jardiniére. He waved away science with a white hand.

"All the work he did during the war," Sam said. "The Manhattan Project. Then after the war all the science policy work for the government. He probably knew everyone of any importance in science. Then the Nobel Prize. That's why his archives ... You say they're staying here? In University Archives?"

"They're there now. Temporarily, at least. There was a moving van blocking the loading dock half the day yesterday. They brought everything down from his office and from his home."

"Temporarily?"

"Until his daughter decides where they should go. The books she had transferred to us a couple of weeks ago now. She seems to think it was months ago. That's the problem, you see. She's furious because I made the decision to keep only the rare books here and have all the others cataloged for the stacks. My god, Sam, it's all just ordinary stuff, for the most part, except he wrote his name in absolutely everything. Maybe underlined a few words. And sometimes there were dedicatory inscriptions from the authors. So, of course, she thinks they're sacred texts. She apparently wanted the whole library kept together. Up here in Special Colletions. As some kind of monument, I guess. Can you imagine. Naturally, I was never told about that. I was not the one she dealt with from the start. First the President, then the Chancellor, than Director of Libraries. And now she's gone to Margaret Sawyer again in a rage, and, of course, Margaret's delighted to have any reason to berate me. I spent an hour in her office yesterday. All this when Margaret has me dealing with another major collection that might be coming in."

"What collection is that?"

"I can't say. I'm sworn to secrecy. Anyway, it's taking enormous amounts of my time. And now I have to deal with June Roth."

Outside, sirens that had risen higher and louder stopped suddenly and Vandersteen stood again to look out the window.

Sam laughed. "They're coming for you, Otto."

"A police car and an ambulance," Vandersteen said, his forehead almost touching the window glass as he leaned to look down. "They've stopped in front of the bookstore."

"The University Bookstore?"

"No, no. Lowell's. In the next block. I can just see it" He turned back to face Sam. "One of those wretched street people passed out on the sidewalk, no doubt. Anyway, Sam, the problem at the moment is I need to have the books appraised. Those I brought up to Rare Books. She's complained about that, too, to Margaret. The wretched woman. You'd think I had nothing else to do. I was hoping you could do it today. What do you think?"

Sam glanced at his wristwatch. "Today? Right now, you mean? I don't know, Otto. Twenty-five books."

"I'm sure Mavis has them up in the reading room by now. You could begin, at least, couldn't you, so I could tell her we've started. I would certainly appreciate it, Sam." He moved around his desk as though he intended to pull Sam from the chair. "At least I'd have June Roth out of my hair for now."

Sam pushed himself up, then bent to rub his knee. "Damn knee," he said. "It'll give out on me one of these days."

"You should consider losing weight, Sam," Otto said. He put his hand lightly on Sam's shoulder. "I understand we'll be seeing you this evening. At Stubblefield's."

"Stubblefield's! Why on earth would I be at Stubblefield's?"

"Because, Sam, he's giving one of his dinner parties and you've said you'd come. Or so he tells me."

"Alma." Sam jerked his briefcase up from where it leaned against the chair. "Good god, she knows ... Well, she can go alone. You'd think she'd get all she can stand of that fool during the day, without having dinner with him, too."

"He has an important announcement to make. You'll be interested, Sam. Really. Alma didn't tell you?"

Sam started toward the door. "Alma never tells me anything. Where are these damn books you want me to see? I have an appointment with Nick."

"An appointment," Otto said with a sarcastic smile. "He's a campus cop. You're going to the terrace for coffee, no doubt. I envy you, Sam. You have no one to harass you, except your wife."

"Alma never harasses me."

"Ha. You just said she's forcing you to Stubblefield's tonight."

"Not 'forcing' me. Where are those damn books? I have other things to do today." He barged through the door to the reception desk, leaving in his wake the smell of stale cigarette smoke indelibly embedded in his clothes. Vandersteen followed on little steps.

From behind the counter, Mavis Martin, telephone pressed to her face again, looked over her shoulder at them. She tucked the phone into her neck and jabbed a finger at a book truck standing just inside the counter gate.

"For gods' sake Mavis," Vandersteen said. He held his white palms up to show the world what he must bear. "Sam, just go into the reading room. Mavis will bring in the truck. Hopefully." He said the last word loudly to Mavis's bent back for she had turned to huddled again over the phone. "I really appreciate this, Sam." He held the tall glass door to the Reading Room open. "If you could just get a start. The hellion daughter is coming in again this afternoon."

"Consider this a personal favor, Otto," Sam said. "Which I will frequently remind you of."

"Undoubtedly," Vandersteen said. He bowed slightly as he backed away.

The individual walnut desks in the Reading Room were empty but for quilted cloth scrolls meant to cradle the opened books and prevent damage to their ancient spines. Sam leaned his briefcase against the leg of a desk near the big windows looking out toward the white dome of the state capitol building. While he waited for Mavis to bring in the books, he went to the window and looked down at State Street. The ambulance and a police car were still pulled onto the wide sidewalk in front of Lowell's Bookstore. A river of students flowed around them as if they were boulders in a stream.

Behind him the glass door crashed against the wooden book truck as Mavis tried to push it through and hold the door open at the same time. With a grunt she forced it through the doorway and with arms stiff and legs pumping began to push it across the carpet like someone rolling a rock uphill.

"That student of mine should've been here half an hour ago," she said, shaking her head at Sam. "This your desk here?"

"That's fine," Sam said. "Just leave it, Mavis. Is that all of them?"

"I guess so. Gladys is the one unpacked the boxes. I'm at the desk, if you need something." She hurried back to where the telephone was waiting.

The top shelf of the book truck was lined by a double row of books in various sizes, bound for the most part in leather. Sam maneuvered the top-heavy truck alongside his desk, pulled up a chair to face the books, and, with a loud clearing of his throat, as if to warn the books he was coming, sat down.

They were fine books, apparently all by Robert Boyle, with Boyle's name in chipped gold letters on the leather spines. Ignoring the desk, Sam opened the books one at a time on his lap in front of his big stomach, studying the title pages, the fly leaves, the inside front covers, leafing through the crisp pages. There were several editions of Boyle's major works: *The Skeptical Chymist, The Spring and Weight of the Air*, and others, all fine copies.

Theodore Roth had had no bookplate but had written his name in black ink at the top right corner of each fly leaf, along with the date he had purchased the book.

"Idiot," Sam grunted. "At least he didn't write on the title pages." He put the books back on the book truck and stood, brushing at smudges on his white pants left by some of the leather bindings.

Mavis Martin sitting at her computer jumped as the big door to the Reading Room rattled open. "Done already?" she said, standing.

"I don't have time for this now, Mavis," Sam said. He leaned his forearms on the marble counter top. "Could you have one of your students photocopy the title pages? I'll work from the title pages first, then come back and look at the books again."

"Well, I don't know about that. You know how he feels about photocopying."

"I'll talk to him. Is he in his office?"

"He just went out again. I think for coffee."

"Coffee! He just got here."

Mavis laughed and pushed a hand at him. "I think he was meeting someone."

Sam knew she was about to gossip. "Alright. Well, I don't have time. Tell him I have to have copies of the title pages when he gets back. I'll come in tomorrow morning again."

ଓ

The elevator door slid open on a crowd of students down from classes on the hill and waiting at the bank of elevators leading to the book stacks and the computer terminals on the upper floors. Sam worked his way impatiently through bodies of young people in shorts and T-shirts. Bulging backpacks hung from their shoulders like permanent appendages on a foreign species. The air smelled of stale bedding where still a trace of perfume lingered and he was relieved to push out the library doors into sunshine on the broad mall between the library and State Historical Society's stone-columned building.

Around the marble rim of a fountain pool in the center of the mall, students sat like clusters of birds around a birdbath, and, on the triangles of lawn between the concrete walks that crossed the mall, young people sprawled with their arms and faces turned to the spring sun in the hope it might be strong enough to turn them brown. A few drunks still slept close together on the grass, curled with their hands between their knees against the cold and damp that lurked like winter hidden a foot below ground. The clusters of crab apple trees in each corner of the mall were just past full bloom. Their pink blossoms had fallen into colored shadows on the grass.

Sam glared at the thrower as a frisbee sailed just over his head. He swung his briefcase up as though about to throw it in retaliation. Inwardly, though, he smiled at the contagious exuberance released in these young people by this fine spring day, with a warm sun in a cloudless sky and the smells of new grass and budding trees competing with those of the newly ice-freed lake he could see now beyond the student Union. He waited with a crowd of impatient students for a break in the cars to cross Langdon Street to the Union and glanced at his wristwatch, wondering if Nick would still be on the terrace. Probably not, at ten-thirty.

Inside the Union he stood in line at the deli counter for coffee, then wound his way through the heavy oak tables filling now with students in the gloomy, pseudo-German interior of the Rathskeller. He held the Styrofoam coffee cup out in front of him like a spearhead to keep students away until he reached the doors sliding open to the limestone terrace facing the lake. The winter-stored red and green and white metal tables and chairs had bloomed again like bright flowers out of the limestone ground. Most were occupied by university people and students. Sam stood searching for Nick, then started toward tables still empty because they were in the thin shade of the young leaves on the oak that anchored the terrace. He had already sat in one of the metal armchairs that was too small for his big body and hopped it closer to the table when he saw Alma at a table in the sunshine listening to a young man who leaned across the table toward her, arms gesturing as though he were outlining the shape of something. Alma was facing Sam and looking toward him over the shoulder of the young man.

Damn, she's seen me. Why isn't she in her class?

Sam half-slumped in his chair and pretended he had not seen her, but Alma stood and waved him to join them. Affecting a weary waddle to show his annoyance, he waded through a flock of impervious sparrows pecking at crumbs a bored student was throwing onto the limestone and stood behind the empty chair at Alma's table, his briefcase propped on the chair's round back. The young man had turned to watch him and stood now, frowning.

"Sam, dear, you remember Audie Thorson, don't you?" Alma said.

"Audie," Sam said, not admitting anything. He held out casually his big hand and the young man seized it and shook it firmly, a handshake he had practiced.

"Pleased to meet you," Audie said, sitting again.

"Audie's Harry's son," Alma said. "Harry Thorson, in Fox Prairie. You met him last year, at Langdon Manor when we were having dinner with Nick. Sit down, Sam. I expected you to be gone by this time."

He looks foreign, Sam thought. Probably from California. Tan skin already. Dark hair. Spanish eyes. Doesn't look like any son of Harry's. Who's that on his T-shirt? Some rock star.

"I got delayed, so I missed Nick," Sam said. He pulled out the chair and squeezed into it, leaning his briefcase against the metal leg. "Did you see him?"

"No," Alma said, "but it's crowded." Alma's graying hair was cropped short in a style that Sam had never liked but which she claimed was "so much easier to care for." It didn't really matter because for Sam there was nothing Alma could do that would make her less beautiful, this woman he had first seen over twenty years ago in a bookstore in New York and had married two years later and loved enough even to leave Manhattan and follow to a place he could never have imagined living. Sam thought if she'd dye her hair no one would ever think she was fifty-five: slender yet, with a broad, firm-skinned face wrinkled only at the corners of the eyes and mouth from frequent smiling; large, dark eyes that showed curiosity, at least, if not always interest, to even the most boring person talking to her. There was a kind of fierceness about her, too, that only Sam knew she maintained as guard against the return of the cancer she had fought eight years ago. On her lavender dress a broach with amber stones glittered in the sunlight, her favorite of all the old jewelry she had kept when her parents had closed the antique store they had owned in lower Manhattan, in the same block as the many bookstores Sam used to haunt. He had asked her only once why all her dresses were shades of purple, and she had said "Because it's my color, is why."

Sam dug the pack of cigarettes out of his shirt pocket, shook one out and laid it on the white enamel of the table while he searched among keys and loose change in his pants pocket for the silver lighter Alma's father had given him the Christmas before he died.

"My first one since breakfast," he said to Alma's disapproving look.

"He'll never quit," Alma said to Audie. "I've given up."

"Would you like one, young man?" Sam held out the cigarette pack.

"Sam!"

"No thanks," Audie said with a puzzled smile. "I don't smoke. I wonder why people say 'young man' all the time to me here. They never did in California."

Ah, California, Sam thought. He knew it. "Well, they're all young out there, aren't they? Or think they are, anyway.

You're from California?" he asked. He blew smoke toward his shoulder. "I thought you were Harry Thorson's son."

"I lived there with my mother until I started school here last year."

"Audie's in my American literature class," Alma said. "We were just discussing Melville."

""You interested in books, Audie?" Sam asked.

"Books?"

"Sam is a bookseller, Audie. Rare books. First editions, that sort of thing."

"I'm working in the bookstore here," Audie said. "Lowell's. Part time, anyway."

"Really," Sam said. He pulled himself up in his chair and looked at Audie as if he had turned into someone interesting. "I don't remember seeing you there."

"I just work nights, mostly. When Alice's not there." He stood up and bent to retrieve his backpack from under the table. "I've got to get back up the hill," he said. "Thanks for the help, Professor Ives."

"Not at all, Audie. We'll have you to dinner one evening."

"Nice to meet you, Mr. Ives."

"He's quite bright, you know," Alma said, watching the boy cross the terrace toward the Rathskeller. She laughed. "His name's Audubon. Wouldn't you know Harry would call his son Audubon."

Sam raised a shoe to his knee and ground out his cigarette butt on the sole, careful to avoid the thin spot. He shifted in his chair and dropped the butt into the pocket of his sport coat, obeying Alma's frequent warning not to litter. Sparrows hurried across the limestone to inspect what might have been thrown by Sam's motion, then flew back to the low stone wall that separated the upper terrace from the larger terrace along the lake shore.

"Speaking of dinners, Professor Ives," Sam said. "What's this about Stubblefield's tonight?"

"We're invited. I couldn't think of an excuse, dear."

"I could have. You should've asked me."

"You weren't there. Alfred asked me in the department yesterday."

"Well, it's the first I heard of it. Otto Vandersteen's the one told me, not my wife."

"I did tell you, dear. You just don't remember. And Alfred is especially eager for you to come. He has a surprise 'announcement,' and he has something he wants your opinion about."

"So I've heard."

"Anyway, just remember that his partner is an awfully good cook. I'm sure he'll have something wonderful."

"I can't smoke there."

"But you can have as much of his single malt Scotch as you like."

"True. I'll need it if 'Roger' is there, too," Sam said.

"Now dear, don't be homophobic."

Sam grunted and removed the plastic lid from his coffee "I'm not. I just don't like Roger. I saw him here on the terrace the other day having coffee with Vandersteen. I wouldn't have thought those two would even know each other."

"Through Alfred, I suppose," Alma said. "Otto will be at the dinner tonight. I imagine he's been at Alfred's before, and met Roger there."

The tables around them were emptying now as students rose in groups to start to the eleven o'clock classes. They flowed up from the lower terrace and around Sam's and Alma's table. Sam had to pull his chair in to keep from being bumped by backpacks. The sparrows had fled into the new leaves of the oak and, waiting to return, chattered like a crowd forced out by a fire alarm.

"Why is it Midwesterners all look so healthy?" Sam said, eyeing a young woman.

"It's the milk, I think," Alma said. "Anyway, they're not all Midwesterners, not by half."

"I saw you earlier, you know, with Stubblefield. Going past the Brew Kup."

"Really? I met him on the way in. He can be so persistent: Alfred. He's quite upset about not being on the search committee to replace Burton More. I really don't know what he thinks I can do about it."

Both were looking at the people around them, their conversation merely habitual.

"You're chair, aren't you? The chair gets blamed for everything."

"Chair of the committee. Howard appointed the committee, not me."

Sam started to reach for his cigarettes, then decided to wait. He folded his hands on the table. "Alma, how well did you know Ted Roth?"

"Ted? Not all that well. We were on the University Committee one year together, and he was on the Library Committee when I was, too, but he rarely showed up for meetings. He was asked to be on everything, I'm sure, being so eminent. Alfred knew him much better than I did."

"Stubblefield? How on earth would he know someone like Roth? A physicist."

"Well, I really don't know. He dropped Ted's name at every chance, though. I think it might have something to do with books. Apparently Ted was a book collector, too. And Roger knew him, as well. Somehow. Better than Alfred did, I believe."

"Roger? He's a clerk."

"Administrative assistant, dear."

"How would Roger know Ted Roth? I didn't even know him."

"I don't know, dear. Why are you so interested in Ted Roth?"

"I've just now seen the books he left to the library. Wonderful collection of Robert Boyle. Otto's asked me to appraise them. I'm curious where he bought them."

Alma stood and smoothed the lap of her dress. "June would know, I should think. You should talk with her. I've got to get back, dear. Office hours."

"His daughter? How do you know her?"

Alma, alongside him, bent to kiss his cheek. "Sam dear, you know her, too. I introduced you last year at the Friends of the Library dinner. And anyway, you must remember her eulogy at Ted's funeral. Sam, that awful tie. I wish you would ... Well, you can talk to her tonight at Alfred's. He's told me his is the first invitation she's accepted since the great man died. Bye, love."

Sam grunted and retrieved the pack of cigarettes from his shirt pocket. He held them in his lap until Alma had time to disappear. Two sparrows flew down to sit on the edge of the table where Alma had been, their miniature claws clicking on the enameled metal as they hopped hopefully toward him. He swung out an arm and they flew away. Out on the dark blue lake a cluster of sailboats from the sport club swarmed in disarray as their novice sailors tried to find the right direction in the light breeze. Someone behind Sam was smoking marijuana and the grassy smell tainted the smoke from his own cigarette.

Pushing himself up out of the chair, he put too much weight on the chair's right arm and almost tipped sideways. His briefcase against the chair leg fell on his shoes. With one hand he shoveled his bushy hair back into some kind of order.

Instead of going back through the Rathskeller, he walked along the glass wall of the cafeteria to the mall between the Union building and the old red brick gymnasium. He crossed Langdon Street in the middle of the block. He leaned a minute against a parking meter to catch his breath after having hurried to beat the car that hadn't bothered to slow for him.

"Damn kids", he said to the parking meter. Just before he reached the corner with State Street, he saw an ambulance turn toward University Avenue, and as he rounded the corner at Walgreens one of the two police cars in front of Lowell's Bookshop began to back off the sidewalk into State Street. A policeman in the bookshop doorway stopped him.

"Can't go in," he said.

"What's going on?" Sam asked.

All the old globe lights hanging from the ceiling like giant marshmallows were on in the bookstore now. Over the cop's shoulder Sam could see four men around Alice's desk.

"Just move on," the cop said. He put the palm of one big hand up as high as Sam's head.

Two of the men by the desk were in police uniform. An older man, hands deep in the pockets of pale blue slacks, wore a tan summer-weight sport coat that even from a distance looked rumpled. The fourth man, in the khaki uniform of Campus Security, Sam knew.

"Nick," Sam called over the cop's shoulder.

"Didn't I tell you to move along?" the cop said. This time he put his hand on Sam's chest.

"Young man!" Sam warned. His face began to redden. He pushed the cop's hand down. He stepped aside to the bookshop's plate glass window and pounded on it, then cupped his hands against the glass to look in. The cop was at his shoulder about to pry him away from the window when Nick Ash came out the door.

"It's alright, officer," Nick said. "I'll talk to him."

"Fascist," Sam said to the young policeman's back. "What the devil's going on, Nick?"

"Let's get out of the way here," Nick said.

A lunch hour crowd of office workers and students had begun to cross Lake Street from the library mall and funnel onto the sidewalk. The two men were surrounded by hungry people hurrying to beat the lines at Pizza Hut or McDonald's or the ethnic restaurants that lined State Street. Nick lead Sam to the back of the police car parked half over the curb. He sat against the rear fender, arms crossed. Almost forty now, his once handsome face showed the anxiety of a man who wasn't certain he had seen the last of the black-dog depressions that had plagued him in the past. His dark hair was damp yet from the swim he took every morning in the campus gym, keeping his body lean, washing away in the sting of chlorinated water, lap after lap, the last-night smell of cigarettes and alcohol, the night thoughts.

Sam had met him when he and Alma had first come to the university.

"Has something happened to Alice?" Sam asked.

"She's dead," Nick said. "They just took her away."

"Good god! I was just there, talking to her. An hour ago. Two hours ago."

"She was murdered. Strangled. Apparently."

Sam's face paled. "But I ... Strangled?"

"With the dog's leash. Al Nielsen's in there. They don't think it was robbery, either. The cash register is still locked."

"Who's Al Nielsen?"

"From the police department. The homicide detective? You met him once. Last year."

"I can't believe this, Nick. Strangled?"

"You saw her this morning?"

"On my way in to campus. She wanted me to look at a book she'd bought."

"Maybe you ought to talk with Nielsen. They think it happened before she'd opened the place. The lights weren't even turned on yet."

Following Nick to the door, Sam lit a cigarette and blew a puff of smoke like a scarf over his shoulder. He deliberately bumped the arm of the young cop standing in the doorway.

"Sorry, young man," he said, grinning.

Detective Alvin Nielsen, in mismatched sport coat and slacks and an orange tie, looked like a Florida tourist dragged off the bus by his wife to see something else he didn't want to see. His hair had retreated to mid-scalp and what was left had started to turn grey a year ago, after he had quit smoking and failed to quit drinking. Shoulder high to Sam and Nick and half the girth of Sam, he met them scowling as he started toward the door with the two uniformed cops behind.

"We're done here," he said to no one. His voice was as hard as wood. He kicked at a row of boxes that had almost tripped him.

"Al, you remember Sam Ives here," Nick said.

Sam stepped from behind Nick and stuck his cigarette in his mouth to shake hands with Nielsen. "I was here earlier," he said.

"Yeah, I remember you from last year," Nielsen said. "Mark Twain."

Sam looked down at his white suit as if it might have stains on it. "Oh," he said. "Well."

He blew smoke at the ceiling.

Nick said, "Sam saw Alice this morning. Right before she opened the place. I thought maybe he should talk to you."

"She had a book she wanted to show me," Sam said.

"What time was that?" Nielsen asked.

"As Nick said, right before she had opened. She hadn't turned the lights on yet. So nine-thirty, I suppose."

"Well, she never did turn the lights on," Nielsen said. "They were out when we got here. Anybody else in here, when you were?"

"No, we were alone. I bought an encyclopedia from her. Actually ..." Sam looked around Nielsen to see if the books were still there. "I was just going to stop to see her again, about the books."

Alice's yellow lab walked slowly past the men and bumped its head against Nick's knee. Nick knelt and took the dog's big head in his hands. "Belle," he said, flapping the dog's ears. "Poor old Belle."

"Where'd the dog come from?" Nielsen asked.

"Probably hiding under the desk." Nick looked up, still squatting beside the dog. "She's kind of shy sometimes. What happens to the dog, Al?"

"How do I know? She have a husband, kids?"

Sam said, "Her husband died a few years ago. They used to run this place together."

"She didn't have kids," Nick said, standing again. The dog sat on his shoe and Nick kept the tips of his fingers on its head. "She's got a sister. Lives in Los Angeles."

"You take the dog then," Nielsen said to Nick. "Can't leave it here. Or else call the dog pound to come get it."

"Me? I've just got an apartment." Nick knelt again to the dog. "What to do with Belle," he said. The dog licked his face.

"Well, you decide," Nielsen said. "Just don't leave it here."

"Detective, about the books," Sam said. "I bought an encyclopedia from Alice this morning. You suppose I could get it sometime today?"

"No way. Nothing goes out of here 'til our people have been through the place."

"It's just in the back room. I could ..."

Nielsen glared at him. "Everybody out. We're locking the place up." He held his arms wide to herd them to the door. "What's your name again?" he asked Sam.

"Sam Ives." Sam dropped his cigarette butt and ground it with his shoe.

"Here, write it down. And your phone number." Nielsen handed him a small notebook and pencil stub. "I'll wanna talk to you later."

On the sidewalk the dog sat next to Nick's leg. "I don't have a leash for her," Nick said. "I'm working yet, anyway."

"Call the dog pound then," Nielsen said. He opened the door on the passenger side of the squad car parked half on the sidewalk and waited for the other cops to mark the door to the bookshop with yellow crime-scene tape. The three men ducked into the car together. Nielsen stuck his head out the window as the car backed into State Street.

"I'll be in touch," he said. "Good luck with your new friend there." He grinned, nodding to the dog.

The old dog sat between Nick in his khaki uniform and Sam in his white suit and looked at the door to the bookstore.

"Great," Nick said. "I don't even have a leash."

"It's hardly going to run away," Sam said. "It looks to me like you might even have to carry it. Let's get a coffee, Nick."

Nick looked at his wristwatch. "I've got to report in. About what happened here."

"It's not a campus thing, is it? I mean, this is a city street."

"No, but I have to report anyway."

"Well, the Brew Kup is just in the next block. Come on. We'll get a sidewalk table, for the dog's sake."

As they moved onto the crowded sidewalk, the dog walked along beside Nick's leg without urging and without looking back, as if it knew already its world was different now. Nick kept looking down at it and smiling.

"That dog likes you," Sam said. "Animals like you, Nick. Our cat thinks you're his true love."

"At least this is a girl," Nick said. "I wonder what the rules are about pets in my building."

&#x2603;

Noon was not rush time at the Brew Kup. Two of the white plastic tables on the wide sidewalk were empty and Nick sat at one with the dog lying on the concrete beside his chair while Sam went in to get the coffee. The other tables, crowded close, were filled with a mix of students and street people. The man at the table next to Nick seemed agitated and held onto his Styrofoam cup with both dirty hands, as though trying to warm them. A cigarette stub managed its own precarious hold on his lips. He mumbled something Nick could not understand.

Sam returned with a miniature cup and saucer and a coffee mug. He held them both aloft as he squeezed his big body into the narrow arms of the plastic chair, then handed Nick the coffee. A UPS truck rocked past, braked, then accelerated again, passing exhaust.

"Charming place," Sam said. He sipped his espresso and lit another cigarette. "How the city has the nerve to call this glorified alley a mall is beyond me. They should never have allowed vehicle traffic. I wrote them a letter about it, you know: the newspaper. So, what do you make of this, Nick? Alice, I mean. Poor woman. I can still hardly believe it." He breathed in the cigarette smoke deeply, as if it were oxygen to him, and slumped as much as the chair would allow. "It must have happened right after I left her. Gives one the creeps. Maybe the guy was even in there and I didn't see him. I wish that Nielsen would have let me take my books. There was a very valuable book in that box, Nick, with the encyclopedia. Alice was being very secretive about it. She bought it from someone last night she said, but she wouldn't say who."

The dog sat up and put one paw on Nick's knee. Nick scratched its ear. He watched a flock of women crowd together to pass between the outside tables and the storefront. They were all talking, except the pretty one. Nick watched her. Most carried packages wrapped with what looked like colored tinfoil tied with wide white ribbons.

Sam looked over his shoulder to see what Nick was watching. "How well did you know her?" he asked, turning back. "Alice." He savored a sip of his espresso and looked down at his tie, brushing it.

"I stopped in there most days," Nick said. "To say hello." He cleared his throat and leaned toward Sam, as if deciding something. "You remember her sister?"

"Her sister? I didn't even know she had a sister till you mentioned it to Nielsen."

"Well, she'd probably left town before you would have known her. It was a while ago, now. Anyway, she called me last night."

"She called you. Why would she call you?"

"We were friends. Anyway, she's back here, in town. She's been staying with Alice."

"Well there you go. You don't have to take the dog after all."

Nick laughed. "She wouldn't want a dog."

Sam studied him. Nick was looking at the dog. "What are you trying to tell me?" Sam said.

"Nothing really. Just I'll have to call her, about Alice. I didn't tell Nielsen. I thought I should do it myself."

"You knew her pretty well? When she lived here."

Nick grinned at Sam. "She's a lot younger than Alice. Her younger sister. She went off to California to be an actress or some dumb thing."

"So. Another of Nick's lady friends. Nick, Nick. So, what'd she call you about?"

Nick shrugged. "Said she just wanted to talk."

"And did you?"

Nick brought the mug up to his mouth and blew on the steaming coffee. "Not really. A little over the phone. I just didn't want to see her again, to be honest. Guess now I'll have to. About Alice."

"Well, I don't envy you that."

"I don't know. The two of them never got along, Alice and Claire. I'm surprised she'd stay with Alice, even. Never thought she'd come back here, a little town like this. Alice said she didn't do very well out there, in Los Angeles. Always writing her asking for money."

Sam said, "Hmm. You think maybe she might have ...?"

Nick laughed. "What? Killed Alice? No way. She doesn't even get out of bed before noon."

"Well, for a special occasion." Sam pushed up in his chair. "I shouldn't make fun of it. Poor Alice. I wonder what'll happen to the shop."

"Why don't you buy it?"

"Are you kidding? Not my kind of books. No, I gave up second-hand bookshops long before I left New York. What do you think happened, Nick? To Alice?"

Nick nodded his head toward the man at the table next to them, still staring into the coffee mug he held cupped in both hands. "There're a lot of strange people on this street, Sam. That time of day, any one of them might have been just coming out of his night trip, walked in there and found some kind of left-over demon he had to kill." Nick reached down and scratched the top of the dog's head. "Belle here probably saw it all, if she could only talk. Why didn't you scare him off, old girl?"

"What are you going to do with the dog?"

"I'll keep her awhile, I guess. See if anyone wants her. See how it works out in my apartment." Nick drank his coffee and started to get up. "I've gotta get going."

"Nick, you suppose you could talk to Nielsen about my books? I'd really like to be able to pick them up. I paid her already. Maybe they'll make a big deal about whether they belong to me or not. You don't happen to have a key to the place, do you?"

"No. Why would I have a key? I couldn't let you in, even if I did. I'll ask Nielsen when I see him again, though. You want to meet for a drink later?"

"Later? Like how later?"

"After I get off. Five or so."

"I would, Nick, but Alma's made this damn dinner date."

"Alright. I'll see you tomorrow, then. Thanks for the coffee. Come on, dog."

The dog jumped up and walked beside Nick's leg into the crowd of people. The dog stopped to smell the corner of a building and Nick looked back and waited. Sam watched them. He wondered what the dog had done when someone had stepped out from the darkened bookshelves behind Alice and slipped the dog leash over her head: Alice clutching at her throat, Alice reaching back over her head, face turning red, plump arms flailing, reaching back to whoever was killing her.

Sam shook his head to chase out the image. With a trembling hand, he lit another cigarette and stood. He touched his back pocket to make sure his wallet was still there. He could still see Nick and the dog working their way toward the campus. He reached down for the espresso cup and took a last sip. He noticed the man at the table next to him was looking at him: red-rimmed eyes sunk under heavy brows. The man wiped his mouth with a dirty, calloused hand and seemed about to say something. Sam turned and hurried up State Street toward home.

# TWO

"No, thanks," Alma said. She had just come home and was looking at the message panel on the telephone. "And you shouldn't either, dear. You always have more than enough to drink at Alfred's, so please don't start now. Did you erase the messages?"

"There were only two," Sam said. "One from Stubblefield reminding us. Other one from Dennis Martin in New York."

"What did he want?"

"Wants to buy a book I have but doesn't want to pay full price."

"Why do you even bother with him?"

"I don't. He bothers with me. Well, I'm having a drink. If we have to drive the *Vehicle*—and to Stubblefield's besides—I need something to start on." Sam, already at the liquor cabinet, an antique oak piece they had brought with them from New York, opened the paneled door and reached in for the Scotch. "Besides, it's been a terrible day for me."

At the sound of the opening cabinet, Walt Whitman jumped down from Alma's wingback chair where he had been sleeping and wound himself around Sam's ankles, purring, back arched.

"Go away, cat," Sam said, pushing it with the side of his foot. The big alley cat looked up at him and meowed.

"Don't give him a drop," Alma said. "He'll be gassy again."

"I don't intend to. You're the one's made him a lush."

"I hope you're going to change, dear." Alma was standing just behind him now, looking through the mail. "You look a little stale for going out to dinner."

"I am stale. An old bagel."

She laughed and dropped the mail onto an end table. "Well, we'd better both change. I need a bath first, if we're going."

"We have an option?"

"No, dear, we don't. I'm not all that eager to go, either. I don't know why people have to have dinner parties during the week."

"We're not in Manhattan anymore."

"Aren't you at least curious about Alfred's exciting announcement?"

"Let's not go, Alma. You can say we're too upset about what's happened to Alice."

"Alice? Alice who?"

"Alice Lowell. You haven't heard?"

"The shop was sealed off when I passed it tonight. Was she robbed?"

"She was murdered. Strangled. And I was there. I talked to her just before it happened. The police have questioned me. You see why we can't go. I'm too upset."

"How awful. But you didn't really like her, you know. You were always complaining. And I know she didn't like you. She even told me once, when I was in there."

"What difference does that make? She's been killed." Sam dropped into his chair. The green leather squeaked comfortably. He held up his glass to Alma. "You wouldn't get me some ice, would you dear?" Walt Whitman sat at his feet, contemplating a leap into his lap.

Alma took the glass. "Look at your hand shake. And you want another drink."

"That's why I want one." He held his hand in front of him and watched it shake. "It's been a very hard day. And it's not over yet. By far. Alice really said she didn't like me?"

"What did the police say?" Alma called from the kitchen. The refrigerator door slammed and she came back with ice clinking in the glass tumbler she handed Sam. "Do they know who did it?"

"No. They think maybe some street person. At least Nick does."

"Nick. Was he there, too?" Alma crossed to the liquor cabinet. "I just might have a martini, as long as you're insisting on drinking."

Except for Alma's upholstered chair, the large living room of their downtown apartment, with windows that looked out on the lighted dome of the state capitol building, was furnished with the mission furniture and arts-and-craft pottery and lamps Sam had been collecting even before he married Alma. The glass-front bookcases on either side of a large oil painting of a Manhattan street scene were filled with novels and the more expensive pottery pieces that had to be protected from a large and careless cat. Between Sam's chair and Alma's, a tall stained-glass lamp stood on a dark oak table. A leather sofa against a wall painted amber faced their chairs, and an oriental rug covered the floor.

Alma sat down with her martini glass held up against the inevitable leap of the cat into her lap. "No," she said, and lifted it even higher as the cat raised a paw toward the glass. "Just go or I'll put you in the den."

Sam lit a cigarette and blew smoke at the ceiling. "If we were in New York now ..." He held up his wrist. "What time is it? If we were in New York now, we could go out for cocktails at Marin's. Take a cab. No *Vehicle* to worry about. Then to dinner at ..."

"Really, dear, you sound like you're in a nursing home," Alma said. She sipped her martini. "Tell me what happened, about poor Alice."

"She was strangled with the dog's leash," Sam said. "Nick's taken the dog, by the way. I think he's going to keep it."

"Strangled in broad daylight? Working in her shop?"

"She hadn't opened yet. I was in there because she wanted to show me a book. Rather a nice book, too. I wanted to buy it, but you know Alice. Always suspected I was putting one over on her. I did buy an encyclopedia, by the way. Eleventh *Britannica*. Always wanted one."

"The police questioned you?"

"Well, not long. I think they might want to talk to me again. Although there's nothing I can tell them. The place was empty when I left." He finished his drink. "Come to think of it, though, Alice did say she heard someone come in. We were in the back looking at the books."

"Good lord. You might have been murdered too. Stop that, Walt." She pushed the cat down.

"Doubt it. Pretty hard to knock off two people at once. I'd have run while he was working on Alice."

"Sam!"

"No, I think Nick's probably right. Somebody thought they could get in the cash register while the place was dark yet and Alice caught him at it."

"Poor Alice. Well, I'm going to take a bath. Change your clothes, Sam."

Sam grunted and looked at his empty glass. "I don't suppose you'd consider going alone, would you?"

Alma placed her martini glass on the rug for the cat to lick. "No," she said, going to the hallway. "And no more to drink until we get there."

Ⰶ

Langdon Manor was built in the early twenties of limestone blocks hauled from a local quarry. Located at the top of Langdon Street, the five-story building had views of the lake and, five blocks away, the soaring white dome of the state capitol, at night turned silver by floodlights. The state legislators had been generous with funds to build what was to be home to many of them while they were in town for legislative sessions: the lobby walls were marble and the floor terrazzo tile; the elevator's door brass and the walls inside polished cherry. The lower floor, partly underground, had contained a bar and a restaurant for the exclusive use of the lawmakers, but they seldom used it, complained of the food, complained, finally, of having to live so close to either too many Republicans or too many Democrats, and the state eventually sold the building to the university. The university converted it to apartments for distinguished (and childless) faculty members. Fifteen years ago the top floor apartment, with three bedrooms and two baths, had been used to lure Alma Ives, whose biography of Emily Dickinson had been nominated for the Pulitzer Prize, away from Columbia.

On the elevator descending, Alma looked down at her lavender dress and brushed the lap. "I hope you're right," she said. "It's still May, you know. I should have taken a jacket."

"You'll be fine," Sam said. He touched his shirt pocket to make sure of his cigarettes. He had changed from his white seersucker to white cotton that was as rumpled as his face. "Do you have the keys?"

"Of course."

The maroon Cadillac with a white vinyl top and white leather seats sat in its outlined lane in Langdon Manor's parking lot. The roof and the hood were littered with the white petals of a near-by catalpa tree.

"That nasty tree," Alma said. She unlocked the door to the driver's side, then, careful not to touch her dress to the dusty fender, brushed away petals clustered like dead butterflies along the windshield wiper. "I wish they'd cut it down. My poor car. I really must take it to the carwash."

"I'm waiting," Sam said from the other side of the car, his hand on the door handle.

Alma had bought the car a month after they had moved from New York, claiming no one in the Midwest could do without an automobile. "They'll think we're communists, if we don't."

"My god, it's a yacht," Sam had said when it was delivered to the parking lot. "You couldn't find a smaller one. How much did it cost?"

"It's a used one, dear. I think it's beautiful."

Sam had argued they should take taxis.

"But what if we want to go out to the country?" Alma had said.

"Why would we do that?"

"Well, to see the scenery, the colored leaves in the fall."

"There're colored leaves in town."

Neither one had known how to drive, but Alma had taken lessons, though Sam had refused. She claimed to be a good driver, but both fenders on the passenger side were crumpled and had not been fixed. And she was afraid to drive on ice, so all winter the car stood like a igloo under snow in the otherwise plowed parking lot.

"What's the matter with it?" Sam asked as Alma ground the motor.

"Nothing's the matter. We just haven't started it in a while."

The interior smelled of stale cigarette smoke. Sam rolled his window part way down and lit a cigarette. Alma's driving made him nervous. In the back seat of a Manhattan cab he had always felt oblivious of danger, no matter how wildly the cabbie drove. Riding with Alma he kept his feet pressed hard on the floor, with sometimes a hand on the dusty dashboard to brace himself should the car two feet in front of them suddenly brake.

The car started. Alma turned the headlights on and drove slowly through the parking lot. A student on the sidewalk hurried out of the way, and she eased onto Langdon Street, both hands on the steering wheel. Mansion-size fraternity and sorority houses lined Langdon. Many students were out in the

early evening, drinking beer on front porches, throwing
frisbees on the wide lawns, walking in groups on the sidewalks
down toward the campus.

"What time is it?" Alma asked. She turned onto Lake
Street and passed the library's loading dock.

"Almost seven," Sam said. "We're late. I hate to be late,
you know. It's rude. They'll already have had drinks."

Alma hurried through a yellow light at the intersection
with University Avenue and joined the rush of cars in the
four-lane thoroughfare that led one-way past the campus.

"You should be in the left lane," Sam said.

"Well, not just yet, really." But she looked back over her
shoulder, flipped the turn signal, and crossed two lanes chased
by someone's angry horn.

College Heights began just beyond the campus. For many
years it had been the first choice to live for the faculty. Its
large, old houses under even older trees, its steep, curving
streets that permitted no short cuts for city traffic, its
nearness to the campus, had made it so desirable that the
houses had become too expensive for all but the most senior
professors. But in recent years, as the old professors had
begun to die off, non-academics with money made from
developing shopping centers or fast-food franchises had begun
to move in. To the horror of their neighbors, some of the
newcomers had torn down the old houses and built even larger
ones that sprawled as close as allowed to property lines and
had garage space for three cars and even the occasional
swimming pool. So sometimes now on summer days the sound
of chain saws cutting down old trees would rip the air as
violently as if a jet plane had suddenly descended to street
level.

Alfred Stubblefield lived in a house designed by an
architect he insisted was famous. "A student of Wright's,"
Alfred claimed. "One of his best. This was one of his early

houses.    Fought  with  Wright—who  didn't?—went  off  to
California and did his major work there."

Built on the slope of the hill that gave College Heights its
name,  the  house  looked  like  a  prairie-style  ranch  with  an
underground  garage  on  the  down  slope.  Tall  windows  set
deeply into the yellow brick front and the roof overhang was so
exaggerated it had begun to sag, making the house look weary.
Severely pruned yews hugged the base of the house on both
sides of concrete walls that protected a stairwell with two
concrete  steps  leading  down  from  the  sidewalk  to  the  front
door.

At the doorway, Sam, glanced back at the car, and said "I
hope  you  remembered  the  emergency  brake."  With  angled
wheels the big Cadillac clutched the curb of the steep street
and seemed to be holding up the three smaller cars parked
above it.

Alma  brushed  the  shoulder  of  her  dress,  suspecting
something might have fallen from the cobweb-laced eaves
above her. "We should have brought wine," she said. "I
completely forgot." She pushed again the mother-of-pearl
buzzer on the doorframe. "Alfred, answer your door. I hate
houses where you can't see if someone's coming or not."

Stubblefield pulled open the door and held his arms wide,
his face anxious. "At last," he said, exaggerating a sigh. "I was
afraid you'd forgotten. You're the last ones, you know."

"Sorry, Alfred," Alma said. She tried to duck past him but
was unable to avoid the big man seizing her shoulders and
kissing her on the cheek.

"Lovely,  dear,"  he  said.  "It's  just  that  Roger's  made  a
chicken thing he refuses to put in the oven until all are here."
He turned to Sam, still in the doorway, and held out a hand.
"Sam, Sam, good to see you. Come in, for heaven's sakes."

He  was  dressed  in  a  brown  suit,  a  paisley  tie,  and  a
yellow shirt with a collar that had collapsed under the weight
of his jowls. There was a perpetually anxious expression on his

face and he frequently put his palm to his forehead as if feeling for a temperature or the dew of perspiration. His flushed complexion made him seem to be blushing. His hair had turned white when he was still young, but it was very full and slightly wavy and he was very proud of it.

The scent of something lemony trailed after him now as he led them down the short hallway into the living room. "Here at last, here at last," he announced to the standing company, holding an arm back in presentation toward Sam and Alma.

In spite of what Sam thought of Stubblefield, he had always liked his house. Built-in bookcases crammed with books filled the wall on both sides of a fireplace of the same yellow brick as the house's exterior. Eight-inch crown molding of golden oak outlined the ceiling. Square pillars of the same oak stood on the half walls of the wide entrance into the dining room. Beyond the dining room table a wall of French doors opened onto a cantilevered terrace that looked down a steep, wooded slope to a dry streambed. But Stubblefield had ruined the bungalow character of the house with a mismatched assemblage of furniture and lamps, from aluminum-frame side chairs with black leather seats to a Naugahyde La-Z-Boy next to the fireplace, a colonial maple coffee table between facing Victorian love seats, and, against one wall, a long red-lacquered cabinet of oriental design whose opened doors revealed a television set and shelves of videos. Sam had always suspected that Stubblefield's taste in furniture depended on who his partner happened to be.

The people in various parts of the room had drinks in their hands and looked as if they had been standing for hours. Out of the mutter of acknowledgments, only Roger Limbert came forward to greet them, bowing slightly twice in front of them, as if to match the Chinese cabinet.

"I'll just put the chicken in, then," he said.

He was a slight man, in his mid-thirties, with narrow shoulders and very thick and well-cared for hair that seemed too big for his face. Sam thought he kept it blow dried to hide the big ears that nevertheless peeked out like rebellious children behind a bush. Under a corduroy jacket, a maroon turtleneck shirt hugged his long neck.

"You remember Roger, of course," Stubblefield said with a nervous half-bow in response to Roger's bow. "Roger's a California boy. Assistant to the Dean now."

"Alfred, don't introduce us, for heaven's sakes," Alma said. "Of course we know Roger." She bent toward Roger to receive a kiss on her cheek. "I'm sure you've made a wonderful dinner, Roger, and you don't look as if you've spent a minute in the kitchen. I'd be frazzled. My, so many guests, Alfred."

"It will be a while for the chicken, I'm afraid," Roger said. "Alfred will get your drinks. I'll just go ..." He touched Stubblefield's padded shoulder as he went by.

"I'll have some of that good Scotch of yours," Sam said at the same time as Stubblefield's "Come and let me introduce ..."

Alma with her bright smile led the way into the room where several obviously relieved people turned to her like flowers to the sunshine. "Well, I know Clarence, of course, and Otto, and ..." she began.

"Alma, Alma." Stubblefield stepped between her and the assembled guests. "Let me. You always think you know everyone. Sam, come here."

Sam put his hand over the pack of cigarettes in his shirt pocket and sighed. He slumped next to Alma to be presented.

"Sam and Alma Ives, everyone," Stubblefield said. "Some of you know them, of course, but I'll introduce you all anyway, just to remind those of you who've forgotten who you've been talking to for the last half hour." He chuckled. "Alma is our star Dickinson scholar, of course. Sam, her husband, sells books. You know Otto from Special Collections, of course. Ella was ill this evening and couldn't come. Otto's warned us already he'll likely have to leave early. Now June Roth you might not know. Daughter of Theodore Roth, the famous physicist? Clarence Biedermann, you know—our partner in crime in the English Department. Margaret Sawyer, Director of Libraries. And this is Mr. Lars Karlsson, head of Karlsson Electronics—I suppose I should say CEO, in today's parlance—in Chicago. There you have it, and I'll explain later why such mixed company. Now where did the young man go?" He looked over his shoulder as if he expected someone to be standing behind him. "He's being shy, I suppose. So, drinks. Sam, you'd like Scotch. Alma?"

"Vodka martini, please."

Polite conversations had been sputtering out of words, like cars out of gas, and the company now smiled in unison at Sam and Alma as if competing to attract them to their group. Near the fireplace Clarence Biedermann stood slightly behind the shoulder of Otto Vandersteen, as if for protection from the much smaller June Roth, who, even with a forced smile on her squarish face, looked as if she might at any minute throw her cocktail glass at the wall. Margaret Sawyer and Lars Karlsson stood broad shoulder to broad shoulder between the facing love seats, Margaret's bulk only slightly less then the professional-athlete physique of Karlsson.

"Help," Sam muttered to Alma out of the side of his grin. But Alma said "Well," and headed toward the Vandersteen group. Sam looked anxiously over his shoulder for his drink.

"You're the fellow'll do the appraisal," Karlsson said.

Sam turned back to look up at the big man, half a head taller, who had crossed the room to him. In his fifties and still handsome, he wore a dark blue suit and grey silk tie over a very white shirt that, amid the general academic rumple of the rest of the company, made him look like someone from another country. His light brown hair had probably darkened since his tow-headed youth. His translucent, almost rosy, complexion seemed out of place on a rugged face dominated by a large and handsome nose.

"Appraisal?" Sam said.

"The Professor said you'd be here tonight. I'm Lars Karlsson." His voice sounded as if it had echoed off the inner walls of his chest before emerging. "Look here, I hope you'll drive up with me tomorrow. I don't intend to spend two hours in a fleet car with these fellows, talking literature. I have a Cadillac, which you'd be comfortable in." His quick glance at Sam's girth seemed to imply "I think."

"Mr. Karlsson," Sam said. "I have no idea what you're talking about."

"You're not from around here, are you. I can tell by your voice."

"I've been from around here a long time now."

"Not native though. New York? I can usually tell."

"I was born in Manhattan, yes."

"You're not a communist, are you? That white suit."

"There are no communists anymore, Mr. Karlsson. Besides, I have a Cadillac."

"Really. You don't look it. What year? Well, Cadillacs aren't what they used to be. You almost have to have a Rolls these days."

Stubblefield came toward them holding up, as if to expected applause, a rattan tray with a tumbler, a martini glass, and a Tupperware bowl of party mix.

"Here you are, Sam. Scotch."

Karlsson put his empty glass on the tray. With a big hand he dug into the party mix. "I could use another, long as we're not eating yet."

Stubblefield's eyes turned to stone. "Yes, well. As quickly as possible." He bowed slightly and headed across the room to Alma.

"Sarcastic little bugger, isn't he." Karlsson brought a fist up to his mouth to nibble on the party mix. "Not used to eating

"He's an ass," Biedermann said. "I've spent the afternoon with him, for gods' sakes. Really, Margaret, is it absolutely necessary for me to go there tomorrow, too? I've been there several times already, since this whole business started."

"Well, it's up to you, of course, Clarence, but you are president of the Friends."

"We'll have to take that damn ferry. I get sea sick. How are you, Sam?" Biedermann held out a hand to shake as if he had just noticed Sam.

"Whatever this is all about, it's getting damn irritating," Sam said. Biedermann's hand felt like a child's in his. "I'm apparently suppose to go someplace tomorrow I don't even know about."

"Which proves Alma can keep a secret," Stubblefield said. "At least since yesterday. She assured me you'd be excited to go, Sam."

"Go where, damn it?"

"I'll just go see what's holding up dinner," Stubblefield said.

Biedermann said, "You told me, Margaret, when I agreed to be president it was only as a figurehead. I wouldn't actually have to do anything."

"Excuse me," Sam said. His hip and knee were aching. He moved around the love seats to join Alma and took a long drink of his Scotch on the way. "I don't suppose I'm allowed to smoke in here," he said. He stood close to Alma.

"No, you're not," Alma said. She squeezed his arm. "Sam, have you met June Roth? June's just made a wonderful gift of her father's books to the library."

The little woman's hand shot up as if released by a spring and Sam shook it.

"I know," he said. "I was just looking at some of them his morning. Very fine books, they are." She held onto his hand too long and Sam had the feeling she was going to try to pull him closer in order to confide something.

"Where was that, you saw them?" she asked. Between Otto Vandersteen and Alma, she looked almost tiny, no taller than the wingback La-Z-Boy immediately behind her. Sam, remembering her father, thought if her physique had come from her mother the sense of energy and authority he felt immediately on shaking her hand surely had come from her imposing father. She had his face, too, a big, square face with a thin nose like an exclamation point over everything she said. He remembered the eloquent eulogy she had delivered at her father's funeral. Even from the back of the crowded church he had heard every word and her voice had never quavered and there had been no sentimentality. Alma had said on the church steps as they were leaving she felt sorry for June, who would be lost without her father. She had accompanied him everywhere, took care of him after her mother had died. She probably wishes she had been on the plane when it crashed.

Sam noticed, after June Roth had let go of his hand, how she clutched the glass of whatever it was she was drinking with both hands, as if to crush it.

"Otto's asked me to do an appraisal of part of the collection," he said. "I was up in the Rare Book Department this morning looking at the books that he'll keep there."

"Now, you see, this is the problem," she said with a tight little smile. She glanced at Otto Vandersteen who quickly put his martini glass to his mouth. "I'd like your opinion of this. I realize my father's collection of the works of Robert Boyle is of great value. He spent many years searching for them. Many happy hours I accompanied him on his trips abroad, to conferences and such, which my mother never cared to do. In London, the first thing he would do was to call from his hotel two of his favorite dealers in rare books to see what they had been able to find for him. So there is no question that those books—you've already seen how fine they are; he never would buy anything shabby—that those books should be in the Rare Book Department. But the rest of his library ... Perhaps it's

my fault for not having made certain of everything before I
gave the books, but it was my intention, my hope, that there
could be a special room in the library with my father's books
and papers all together, where they could be studied as a
whole, as a part of history. Now the correspondence is in the
Archives, I understand, and the Boyle collection is in the Rare
Book Department, and the rest–thousands and thousands–
God knows where. It's really very distressing. Not my
intention at all."

"I've told June ..." Otto began.

"I know, I know," June said, "some of the books are not
rare. But don't you think, Mr. Ives–I'd like your opinion of
this–that a reconstruction of my father's study, the place
where so many of his important ideas were developed, that
any scholar working in such a room–and they will, you know,
before long, be studying so many of the things he did,
especially his work with the government. And even if some of
the books are not rare, the fact that they have my father's
signature in them, that many of them even have his jottings, it
just seems to me that to mark them up with call numbers and
library stamps would just be a crime. And of course people will
be able to charge them out then, like any ordinary book, and,
good lord, who knows what will happen to them in some
student's room. Coffee spilled. Cigarette burns." She paused to
catch her breath.

"June, where would we find such a room?" Vandersteen
said. "If every donor ... if Mr. Karlsson there were to ask us–
and we're talking about every bit as many books–he could ask
with just as much justification to have a separate room for his
grandfather's books."

"Otto, who was his grandfather?" June said. "I mean,
really Otto: some manufacturer in Chicago? It's not the same
at all."

"So that's the big secret," Sam said. "Karlsson's giving
books?"

"Perhaps you could have a caged off area in the general stacks," Alma suggested, "where her father's books could be non-circulating?"

"A cage!" June cried. "That's not my vision at all. No, no. I had pictured donating even the furniture from the study. His wonderful desk. It was a gift from the Danish government, you know, when Father was there just before the war. He'd been working with Bohr, on ..."

"Well, June," Otto said, "I've really done all I can about it. It's Margaret over there you should be talking to. She's the Director of Libraries, not me."

"I would give the rug, too. It's Persian. Father got it ... well, it would look lovely on the parquet floors you have up there. And his portrait. Not the Audubon plate of finches, though. That was a gift he gave to me. An original, from the great folio edition. Framed beautifully. What is your opinion, Mr. Ives? I would be interested to know. There's also my father's papers, which I understand are now in the university's archives. If the papers could be brought together with the books all in one room, with the furniture, the portrait. That was my vision. I'm afraid it's rather a mess now. There were ten autographed copies of his autobiography. At least ten."

"Well, I'm a bookseller, Miss Roth," Sam said. "I'd look at it differently from a librarian."

"Sam would want to sell everything," Alma said, laughing.

"Oh no. I couldn't sell anything. Unless as a unit. Perhaps I should have tried other institutions that might have been willing to keep everything together. Or the Library of Congress, since he did so much governmental work."

"Come to dinner everyone," Stubblefield announced in a loud voice. He held out his arms in a semicircle to gather them all in. "Now where did Mr. Karlsson go? Ah, here he is."

Karlsson came from the hall, followed by a young man.

"And you've found Audie," Stubblefield said. "Wonderful. So we're all assembled."

"Couldn't reach my daughter," Karlsson said. "This fellow I found on the couch in your study reading says he's sure she's coming. Hate to start without her." He looked down at Audie, chest-high to him, as if wondering whether there was any brain at all hiding under Audie's thick hair.

"Well, we'll keep something aside, should she come," Stubblefield said. "Roger has everything on the table. Audie, step out here to meet everyone."

"I already have," Audie said, grinning. "You introduced me to everybody when I came, and I already know Professor Ives and Mr. Ives."

He was wearing new Levis that looked stiff enough to rasp when he walked, a white shirt, and a tan sport coat with some kind of logo stitched in red over the breast pocket. He didn't seem at all bothered by being the only young person in the room, and, in fact, Sam thought, seemed almost to be studying the others. His hands were plunged deep in his pockets and his broad shoulders were slightly hunched, as if to shrug off the fact that he was remarkable.

"Professor Ives will wonder why I'm not working on that paper I owe her," he said.

"Audie, what a surprise," Alma said. "I wouldn't have expected you here."

"He was suppose to bring my daughter," Karlsson said.

"You never know with Karla," Audie said. "She's the one invited me. Her roommate said I should go ahead, she'd meet me here."

"And how's she going to do that? She doesn't have a car," Karlsson said.

"I don't, either," Audie said. "We were going to walk. It's not far from campus."

Stubblefield tried snapping his fingers but his skin was too moist. "Come, everyone. The food's getting cold."

They moved through opened French doors into a small dining room almost filled by a long oak table and high-back chairs. A stained-glass chandelier shone amber light onto carefully set blue-flowered china, crystal goblets and wine glasses, silverware with bone handles. A platter of rolled chicken breasts steamed at one end of the table, bowls of asparagus and oven-browned potatoes at the other. Roger stood at the head of the table nearest the kitchen door, hands intertwined over his chest as if he were about to say grace.

"How elegant," Alma said.

From behind, Audie touched Sam's shoulder and whispered, "Can I sit next to you, Mr. Ives?"

The guests had bunched together like flotsam near the doors.

"There's no special seating arrangement," Stubblefield said, laughing. "Except for me." And he moved to the head of the table, pressing his big stomach with one hand to pass the backs of several chairs. "And the cook, of course, near the kitchen." He held out an arm to Roger, who, frowning, claimed the other end chair. "But Mr. Karlsson should sit next to me here, the place of honor. And Alma, why don't you sit here, across from him, and Sam next to Mr. Karlsson. Margaret across from Sam. Clarence and Otto next to Roger. Margaret next to Alma. And that leaves Audie and Ms Roth for there." He went up on his toes to point out these last places.

Sam put his arm around Audie. "Sit by me, kid," he said, and pulled the chair out for him.

"There's no place for my daughter," Karlsson said.

"We'll squeeze her in right here, next to me," Stubblefield said. "Should she come." He remained standing amidst the general confusion of several people moving around each other to their places at the table.

"Well," Roger said, pulling his chair under him. "I hope you all haven't spoiled your appetite on Alfred's hors d'oeuvres". His lips spread into a little smile as he looked down the table at Stubblefield. Behind him, OttoVandersteen slouched toward his doom next to June Roth.

Stubblefield tapped a spoon on his water goblet, even though everyone was already looking at him. "Well, I would imagine you are all wondering why I have assembled such a diverse group. Those of you who don't already know, of course." Stubblefield's voice, when he was the center of attention, rose to a point where it did not seem likely it could be coming from such a big body. His forehead was damp and he seemed a little out of breath. "Well, it is to announce a most wonderful gift from our Mr. Karlsson here."

Static cracked under Roger's turtleneck as he cleared his throat at the other end of the table. "Alfred, wouldn't it be better to make your announcement after we've eaten? A little after dinner speech for you. I'm afraid the chicken will be cold."

Sam thought his tone as binding as ice.

"Oh." Stubblefield looked chastised. "Perhaps you're right."

But Karlsson jumped to his feet as Stubblefield sat. "Nonsense," he said. "Why do you think we're all here? To eat chicken? This isn't a done deal yet, by a long shot, but as Al here says, I'm prepared to make a totally free gift of my grandfather's library to the university."

Out of the corner of his eye Sam saw the man's big fingers pinching nervously the hem of his suit coat and wondered if he was nervous in front of a table of academics.

"One of the things it depends on," Karlsson continued, "is how much it gets appraised at, which, I understand, is what Sam here is going to do. I've been told by people in Chicago it's worth several million, at least. Now, I can tell you to the dollar what a big generator is worth, but books are something I know nothing about. Don't even like to read 'em." He smiled as if he expected laughter. "Don't have the time. And the other thing is who pays for the appraisal. I'm told I have to do that, which seems to me ridiculous if I'm already giving you guys millions of dollars worth of books. Anyway, the Chancellor this afternoon said there might be a way to work around that. So we'll see. So anyway, that's the announcement." He sat down again more decisively than was necessary. "Now we'll have something to talk about at this dinner."

Margaret Sawyer leaned over her plate, which thankfully, Sam thought, had nothing on it yet, and said, "Well, I do think we should have a little applause for Mr. Karlsson." And she clapped her hands until the others, except for Sam, patted theirs. "It would be a really wonderful treasure for our library." She looked down table at Vandersteen. "Otto is going to have a great deal to do, what with two such great collections coming to us almost at the same time. He's been up to the estate several times already, haven't you, Otto."

"Well, there's a red and a white wine," Roger said, filling his glass with white, "which I won't really vouch for. Alfred picked them out. I think that dish is not too hot to pass, Alfred, so why don't you start the chicken at that end. I hope it will be alright. I really didn't follow the recipe too closely. Added a few things of my own. And we'll just start the asparagus at this end."

"It looks delicious, Roger," Alma said.

"Well, Karlsson," Sam said, "tell us about this collection I'm suppose to appraise tomorrow without having been asked if I would or not."

Karlsson looked sideways and down at Sam as he dropped a rolled chicken breast onto his plate. "Oh? No one told you? Al here said you're the only one in town could do it."

"Well, that's true," Sam said. "But it's the first I've heard about it."

"It's my fault, dear," Alma said. "Alfred asked me this morning to ask you if you'd be available to do an appraisal. Although he did mention it rather casually, and didn't tell me anything about it. And I knew you would be, so I said yes."

"Well, I wanted it to be a surprise," Stubblefield said, looking for the right potato to spear from the bowl Alma had just handed him. "I didn't tell anyone the details. It's really quite a coup, you know."

Karlsson pushed his chair back so he could turn sideways to Sam. "Look here, Sam, you're going to do this, aren't you? I want this settled pretty quick. It's been way too long already. I'm planning to sell that island. And we have to talk about your charges, too, if I'm going to end up paying for this."

"Island?" Sam said.

"You don't know anything about this, do you?" Karlsson said. He looked accusingly at Margaret Sawyer who was holding down a chicken roll with her fork while she removed toothpicks and string from it.

"I told you I didn't," Sam said. "So tell me. What's this about an island?"

"Surely you've heard of the Karlsson collection, Sam," Stubblefield said. "A book man like yourself. I've been to see it three times now, Otto and I, in darkest secrecy of course. Margaret wanted my opinion as to whether we should pursue it or not."

Karlsson scowled at Stubblefield. "Pursue it? What do you mean, pursue it? You're not hunting rabbits, you know."

Margaret said, "We just needed to know whether it would be right for our library, Mr. Karlsson. Whether we might already have many of the books."

"You already have a set of the Audubon folios, huh." Karlsson sliced his chicken roll in half. "Look here, Sam, my grandfather was nuts about these old books. He started buying them back in the thirties, right after his company got established and he started making lots of money. Kept them right there in his office in the factory, lining all the walls like it was a library or something. Had this big case with a glass top just as you came in the room, with this Audubon folio opened up so you could see the turkey or the eagle, or whatever. He kept showing us kids the 'folio', he called it, like it was the greatest thing in the world to own. Four of them, he had."

"Oh, I have an original Audubon print, Mr. Karlsson," June Roth said. "A folio plate of finches my father gave me for my birthday, not long before he died. All hand colored. I'm so fond of finches, you know. I have several pairs."

"Anyway," Karlsson said, annoyed, "the old man bought so many books—must have spent half his money on them—that he ran out of room in his office. He had bought this island up off the tip of the Peninsula we used to go to on vacation when I was a kid and he decided to build this estate up there. He even moved to it full time after he retired. I never spent much time there because I started working young, running the business after my own dad died."

"It's a marvelous collection, Sam," Stubblefield said. "You'll be bowled over. Some wonderful natural history books, a Coverdale bible, tons of Dickens, a lot of old science stuff."

June Roth said, "My father was a passionate collector, as well, Mr. Karlsson. In fact, he used to compete with your grandfather for some things. I remember him telling me whenever a dealer had sold anything by Robert Boyle before he got his order in it probably went to 'old man Karlsson.'" Between forefinger and thumb she swung a glass of red wine back and forth over a plate full of food. "Did you know my father? Theodore Roth? I should give you a copy of his autobiography before you go. *Booked for Life*, he called it. He so loved books, from childhood on. There are even some of the books he had as a child still in the collection. He won the Nobel physics prize, you know."

"June has just very generously given her father's books to the library," Margaret said.

"Well, it's not entirely settled yet," June said. She gulped some wine.

"That so," Karlsson said. "What's it worth?"

Otto Vandersteen leaned forward at the other end of the table and said, "The very valuable part of the collection is being appraised now, by Sam, for the Rare Book Department."

"Now, you see, that's the problem," June Roth said. "The whole library is very valuable. I just can't get people to understand that. Mr. Karlsson, I would advise you to get a commitment as to what they will do with your books, to honor your grandfather, before ..."

"I don't give a damn about honoring my grandfather," Karlsson said, chewing. He swallowed. "Fact is, I need a tax deduction after selling that island and the house there. Library can do what it wants with the books."

"I hope the chicken isn't cold," Roger said.

"Everything is absolutely delicious, Roger," Margaret said. "What a talent you have."

"Well, Sam," Karlsson said, "are you on board for tomorrow?"

"How can I refuse?"

"We'll hammer out your fee in the car on the way up there."

Plump little Biedermann half rose in his seat and sat again. "Perhaps Sam can take my place as representative of the Library Friends. He's on the Friends board, after all. Do we really need three of us up there?"

"Clarence, Clarence," Stubblefield chided. "Always trying to get out of things, aren't we." He smiled slyly.

Audie leaned next to Sam's shoulder. "Mr. Ives, I wanted to talk to you about Alice dying," he said.

Alma said, "Mr. Karlsson, would there be any Emily Dickinson in your grandfather's collection?"

"Who?"

"The poet."

"There's lots of poetry stuff. My grandfather even thought he was a poet himself. If you can imagine that. Paid to have one of his books published once. Embarrassing to read it."

The doorbell rang almost as loudly as a classroom bell, startling them all.

"That fool bell," Roger said. "When will you ever replace it?" He glared down the table at Stubblefield. "Doorbells should be melodic, don't you think?" he said to Vandersteen next to him. "Not something from a fire station."

"Roger, would you mind?" Stubblefield said. He held his arm out toward the door.

Roger put his hand on Biedermann's shoulder. "Clarence will go, won't you, Clarence. I'll just check on the coffee."

Biedermann rose, blushing. "Surely," he said, and went through the living room, tugging at the seat of his pants.

"My daughter, finally," Karlsson said. He hopped his chair closer to Sam and pushed at Stubblefield's plate. "Make room for her there, Al."

Sam turned to Audie. "What about Alice?"

Audie spoke softly to Sam's shoulder. "I was working last night–in the store?–and she came in with boxes of books in her car trunk she wanted me to go out and get."

"Really," Sam said. "Was there a *Britannica?*"

"A what?"

"The encyclopedia. Is that what she brought in?"

"I don't know. I didn't look. There were a lot of paperbacks. I guess a couple boxes had some green books in, like a set or something. Anyway, I'm kind of worried about the cops right now. I'm scared they think because I worked there I might know something about her getting killed."

Karlsson rose from the table like someone jumping out of water. "What're they doing out there anyway?" His chair was too heavy to push back and he turned, his knees against it, as Biedermann returned followed by a young woman. "Well, I don't believe it. She really is going to school here. I was beginning to think it was all a hoax. Everyone, this is my daughter, Karla."

"I'm really really sorry," Karla said, smiling. "I had an exam this afternoon and afterward there was this demonstration on the library mall, and ... Well, I hope I haven't caused lots of problems."

She was very pretty. Her reddish brown hair was cut short in little ducktails, her eyes were light brown and happy, her skin tight over broad cheekbones and ruddy, as if she had just come in from the cold. Unlike her massive father, she was quite short and would have seemed almost fragile except for a sense of excitement, of enthusiasm that made almost everyone immediately aware of her. She wore blue jeans and a dark red blouse that Sam thought she had probably grabbed from the closet at the last minute as she hurried to change clothes.

"Not at all, not at all," Stubblefield said, rising. "Come sit here, by your father. I'll just go get a place setting for you, and find a chair. We weren't sure you were coming anymore, dear, don't you know."

"Everything looks so good," she said. "I'm starved. Hi, Dad. Sorry to be late." She made a quick smile in pretended apology.

Karlsson swung his heavy chair to the end of the table, next to Stubblefield's. "Just sit here, honey. I'll get a chair from the living room."

Audie was looking up at her, and Karla put her hands on his shoulders and bent to his ear. "Are you really mad at me? Kelly said you were mad."

"I waited fifteen minutes," Audie said. "I didn't think we should both be late."

"It's a good thing I knew the way." She looked up at the others, as if seeing them for the first time. "I don't know any of you, do I? Except Professor Ives. I'm in your American literature class. Audie thinks you're the best teacher he's ever had. I loved it yesterday when you read that poem."

Alma said, "Well, thank you, dear. Aren't you a charmer. Let me introduce you." She started with Sam and went around the table, all nodding when named, with varying attempts at smiles.

Karlsson came back empty handed. "Nothing out there I could sit on," he said. "Sit down, honey. No use both of us standing."

Stubblefield returned from the kitchen, dragging a small chair and holding up a plate with silverware sliding on it as he walked. "This chair will just fit on the end, and it's just right for you, dear. Clarence, pass the chicken down here. I hope it's not cold. There you are, dear. Would you like some wine?"

"She doesn't drink," Karlsson said. He pulled the big chair back next to Sam.

"Dad. I'll have red, please. Well, everybody go on talking. I feel like I've interrupted everything."

Roger stood at the end of the table surveying the dishes. "Would anyone like seconds? Otto, start the potatoes around again. And the asparagus."

Alma said, "Your father was just telling us of the wonderful gift he's making to our library."

"I know," Karla said. "Great Grandpa's books. I wanted them all myself. They're so beautiful. Especially the bird books." She pushed at her father's shoulder. "But he just thinks of taxes."

"They practically fill a whole house," Karlsson said. "A big house. It's silly to even talk about it. You're not even out of school yet."

Sam turned to Audie. "I want to talk to you later. After we get done here. We'll give you a ride home."

"And he wants to sell the island, too," Karla said. "My beautiful island we went to every summer when I was little. And he doesn't even need the money. Wait 'til you see it, Audie. We're going with tomorrow, when they go look at the books."

"First I heard of it," Karlsson said. "You have classes."

"Not Thursdays. Anyway, just one."

"I can't," Audie said. "The police told me I shouldn't leave town."

"Audie," Karla said, shocked.

"Mrs. Lowell was killed this morning, where I work, and the police think maybe I did it."

As if a button had been pushed they all started talking at once and then stopped just as suddenly.

"That's ridiculous, young man," Sam said. "Just because they want to talk to you doesn't mean anything. I know for a fact they think some street person did it."

"But I didn't know anything about it," Karla said. "That nice Mrs. Lowell? Why didn't you tell me, Audie?"

"I couldn't exactly find you today, could I."

Stubblefield cleared his throat loudly. "Oh come now, we've managed to avoid this awful topic all evening. Sam, I have to show you what I bought, before you go. A first *Bleak House*, absolutely perfect, in parts."

"That so. Who'd you buy it from?"

"That's a secret. I'm not telling."

"Well, I don't do anything with English literature anymore anyway."

From the end of the table Roger said, "Why doesn't Clarence tell us about his ... his 'research' trip to Spain? It must have been a wonderful trip, Clarence. All those Hemingway places. And your son went with, I understand."

Biedermann's round face, so easy to blush when attention was called to him, went white instead. "Well I ..." he stuttered. "I ... It was very fruitful, that trip. I found some letters ... an old friend of Hemingway who died ... I ..."

"Alfred tells me you had an NEH grant," Roger said. "Isn't it rather difficult to get grants these days for someone so over-studied as old Ernie?"

"Well, if you have a good proposal ..." Biedermann started. He pushed the remains of his chicken around his plate with an upside down fork.

"And your son? He enjoyed the trip? His first time in Spain?"

Biedermann looked up at him and didn't answer.

"Bierdermann," Otto Vandersteen said, "have you ever tried to get into Hemingway's place in Cuba? I understand there's a treasure trove there the government won't let anyone see."

"Yes, that's true," Biedermann said. "No, I haven't tried." He looked as if he was about to cry.

"Did you see the piece in the paper the other day about the Faulkner letters stolen from the University of Texas?" Alma said. "A supposedly respectable scholar. Fortunately, they've gotten them back."

"Have you ever had a theft, Otto?" Roger asked. He had a slight smile on his face and looked around the table as if he had just given a cue for an amusing story.

"Of course not," Vandersteen said. "Not since I've been curator, anyway."

"I should think it would be quite easy to filch something. Especially for the staff, Otto. Slip something in your pocket, get rid of the catalog cards. No one would ever miss most things, I would imagine. Do you trust your staff, Otto?"

"Don't be ridiculous." Vandersteen hopped in his chair as if starting to get up, then sipped his wine.

Audie said in a voice that cracked a bit from not having spoken out loud yet, "My father's going to leave all his papers to the Rare Book Department, he says."

"Audie's father is a distinguished local writer," Alma said to Karlsson. "Harry Thorson? He's naturalist, poet, novelist, just everything, isn't he Audie. He lives just west of here, in a little town on the river. Some day this summer we must drive over with you, Audie."

Karla said. "Audie and I went there last week, on the bus. It's a cute little town. Fox Prairie. And the river is so beautiful. We saw eagles even, didn't we Audie."

"Look here, Stubblefield," Karlsson said, "what's the plan for tomorrow? Sounds like we've got an army going up there. I hope you've made arrangements about the boat."

"Clarence has. Haven't you, Clarence?"

Biedermann said, "I've reserved a van from the car pool. I hadn't counted on your daughter, Mr. Karlsson, or the young man here, but there should be plenty of room."

"I'm not riding in a damn van," Karlsson said. "I'm driving my own car. Karla and her fellow can come with me. And Sam. What about the boat? Is that fellow Stroud taking us?"

"Yes. We're to meet him at the pier in Rock Harbor at one."

"You have to take a boat?" Alma asked.

"You should come with, Alma." Stubblefield put a hand on her lavender shoulder. "It's a lovely place. The house is magnificent. I've been there three times now."

"Oh yes, Professor Ives," Karla said. "Come. It'd be fun to have you with. I'll give you a tour of the whole island. It isn't all that big. And there are hundreds of deer and other things."

"Alma doesn't like boats," Sam said. "Even ocean liners. I wanted to take the QE II to London once, but she thought we'd hit an iceberg."

Karlsson laughed. "No icebergs in Lake Michigan, last I heard. Although my grandfather would probably have imported one in if he'd thought of it. Loved snow and ice, that old man."

"It's not like a rowboat, Professor Ives," Karla said. "You can walk around on it, like a tugboat, with a cabin and an inside motor."

"I just keep thinking of things lurking down there," Alma said, "when I'm on the water. Things you can't see that suddenly whoosh up and grab you."

"The boat *is* rather like the one in *Jaws*," Biedermann said.

"It's a fifteen minute trip," Karlsson said. "Nothing to make a fuss about. Are we done here?" He looked around the table.

Roger stood up at his end. "How many would like coffee?" He collected plates and piled them on his own. "Six coffees? I'm afraid there's no desert. Alfred didn't give me enough warning."

The table erupted in rising people, pushed-back chairs, discarded napkins, the clattering of silverware on china.

"I'm afraid all this is taking away from my father's wonderful library," June Roth said to Otto Vandersteen as they moved in a crowd to the living room.

"I wouldn't worry," Vandersteen said. "We'll still have to get the whole Karlsson thing down from that damn island. Could take months."

Stubblefield pinched Sam's elbow. "Come see the Dickens, Sam. I'm so excited. I usually can't afford them, you know." He bumped Sam away from the others as if separating a steer from the herd, and lead him to the bookcase on the right of the fireplace. He pulled from the shelf a thick box made to look like a book with a crimson leather label on the spine, *Bleak House* lettered in gilt above by Charles Dickens. "Let's just put it down here," he said, and carried it like a baby to the end table next to the La-Z-Boy recliner. He opened the hinged lid of the box and lifted out a stack of fascicles in light green paper wrappers, the top wrapper typeset in ornate Victorian letters. "Isn't it beautiful? Have you ever seen a better copy? I'm so excited."

"Nice," Sam said. He leaned down to it as if it were under glass. "Pretty hard to get these things in parts today. What'd you pay for it?"

"Not telling."

Sam tapped a square stain on the inside lid of the box. "Was there a bookplate here? You shouldn't remove bookplates, you know. Provenance, and that."

"I didn't. There wasn't one. Isn't it beautiful, Sam?"

"Probably got it from Watson in San Francisco. He's the best for Dickens in parts these days. Not cheap, though, from him."

"Not telling. Not telling." Stubblefield picked up the pile gently and put it back in the box. "Not telling," he chanted as he carried it back to the bookcase.

"I need a cigarette," Sam said. "Or a drink." He saw Audie and Karla listening to Karla's father. Audie was watching Sam and as soon as Stubblefield carried his book away he came over to him. He looked like he didn't belong in the clothes he was wearing: the new Levis and tan sport jacket, white shirt, like a kid whose mother has made him wear new clothes she had bought without him being there. Sam smiled. He liked the kid already. He certainly didn't look like his burly, blustering father.

"You don't think I need to worry about the police, then?" Audie asked. He kept his hands in his pockets and hunched his shoulders.

"They talked to you already?" Sam asked.

"I was in my last class today and this cop called me out of the room. Another guy there in the hallway in just regular clothes told me Alice was killed and asked me a lot of questions. When did I see her last, all that. Then he told me they might want to talk to me again."

"They're just talking to everyone they can think of now, that had anything to do with her. Did Alice stay, after she brought those books in last night?"

"No. She had her car parked out there on the curb where she wasn't suppose to. She just left after I got the books from the trunk."

"So you closed up the place then?"

"Yeah. I always do at night."

"You have a key then?"

"Sure."

"I bought this encyclopedia from her this morning, she was going to drop off for me. Which she can't now, of course. Maybe we could pick it up after we get out of here tonight."

"Well, I guess that would be alright."

"I already paid for it. Here, I can show you the receipt."

"No, I believe you. It's just ... Well, I don't like to go in there, you know, where she was killed like that. And maybe we could get in trouble with the police."

"Nuts. We're not breaking in or anything. You've got the key. Did Alice tell you last night who she got the books from?"

"No. She was in a hurry, I guess."

Stubblefield, returning to them, said, "I don't know why you've decided to exclude literature from your stock, Sam. It's so much more interesting than all that old science stuff you sell. Who would ever read that anymore. It's not like a novel, is it? Timeless."

Roger raised to them a red lacquered tray on which several coffee cups trembled. "I've forgotten which of you wanted coffee," he said.

"Roger, you're shaking," Stubblefield said. "For heaven's sakes, put the tray down before you spill."

"How about some of that Scotch of yours instead, Alfred," Sam said.

Biedermann had followed Roger from the kitchen and was standing behind them now, red faced.

He stepped up and stopped abruptly. "Alfred. I'm afraid I have to leave early. I have a class in the morning I haven't prepared for yet."

"Oh, I'm sorry," Stubblefield said. "What's the plan for tomorrow, then, Clarence?"

"Well, those of us going in the van will meet at the car pool at ten. You know where that is?"

"Yes, of course. Will you drive again?"

"I suppose I have to. No one else has a permit. Thank you for dinner."

"What's the matter with him?" Stubblefield said, as Biedermann made his way through people to the door. "Roger, were you teasing him again? Well let's see, Scotch you said, Sam." He stayed for a moment, frowning as he watched Roger move away to offer coffee to the others. "Of course. I'll just get some."

Sam said, "What about it, Audie? Can you let me in the store to get my books?"

Audie glanced at Karla and her father. "I guess so. Maybe Karla will have to come, too. She might get mad if I don't take her home."

"That'd be alright. We can drop you both off wherever you live after we get the books."

Audie looked over Sam's shoulder at the bookcases on both sides of the fireplace. "You people out here sure like books," he said. "My Dad's got books all over the house in Fox Prairie, and Professor Stubblefield ... this is practically a library."

"They didn't have books in California?" Sam said, smiling.

"Not that I noticed so much. Mr. Ives, I was wondering, I'm going to have to find a different job, now that Alice is ... well. You think you might need someone in your store?"

"Store? No, kid, I don't have a store. I sell books out of my house, through the mail. Rare books. Not just the kind of second hand books Alice had."

"No kidding. That sounds like an interesting way to make a living."

Stubblefield returned with a tumbler of Scotch. There was a sudden silence in the room as everyone simultaneously ran out of conversation. Sam raised his glass in simulated toast, as if he himself had managed to quiet them all.

"Would anyone else like an after dinner drink?" Stubblefield asked. "Alma? You always like a drink."

"No thank you. I'm the one driving. Sam, I wish you hadn't started on that. We have to be going."

Sam gulped the Scotch. "Done," he said.

"Alma, it's so early yet," Stubblefield said.

Karlsson said, "You're riding with me tomorrow then, right Sam?"

"Whatever. Better a Cadillac than a van."

Sam and Alma leaving gave the others an excuse to leave as well.

"Why did I bother with coffee?" Roger said as they all moved toward the entryway, bumping against each other at the door, making compliments and thank yous, their clothes carrying the smells of cooking.

"What hotel are you in, Karlsson?" Sam asked. "Case I need to get in touch with you."

"I don't know the name. Right across from where that woman was killed this morning. Noisy as hell all night long. Drunk students in the parking lot."

"Campus Inn. Audie, you're coming with us, right?"

"Audie's deserting me, Dad," Karla said.

"You ride with me, honey. Hell of a date you are, young man."

Audie looked down at his shoes. Out on the sidewalk he talked alone with Karla while the others all climbed into their cars.

"Hope I'm not breaking up anything," Sam said, turning to look to the back seat as Audie slammed the door.

"I don't know why she's mad," Audie said. He sat forward with his arms on the back of the seat between Sam and Alma. "She's the one stood me up in the first place."

"Now Audie," Alma said. "No young lady likes to be dropped off at her dorm by her father." She stepped carefully on the gas but the car did not move. "What's wrong now?"

Sam reached over and released the emergency brake. "It works better without the brake on."

"Oh, I forgot I did that." She started slowly again, moving out into the lane and up the steep hill. "I always have a hard time getting out of this place," she said, leaning forward and clutching the wheel with both hands. "The streets curve every which way."

Sam shifted his weight to look back at Audie. "You've got that key, I hope."

"Yes. In my wallet. It's for the back entrance."

"You have to get in the right lane, Alma," Sam said. "Pretty soon. You're going a little fast aren't you? Alma used to drive cab when we lived in New York, Audie."

When they reached Lake Street the block was parked full with the cars of students at the library or in the bars on State Street. Alma pulled into the loading zone behind Walgreens.

"I'll just wait for you two," she said.

"Where's the back entrance?" Sam said as he pulled himself out the door. "I don't think I've ever been in the back."

"Follow me," Audie said.

A concrete walk lit by a dim, insect-crusted bulb under a metal disk led past two overflowing dump bins behind Walgreens to the back door of Lowell's. Old green paint had cracked and scaled like dried mud on the door. Audie bent to find the keyhole and struggled to insert the key. Sam's shaking hand shone over Audie's shoulder the weak beam of the flashlight he had taken from the glove compartment.

"Alice always told me to lock the dead bolt on the front door and go out this way," Audie said. "But this stupid key ..."

He shook the doorknob and twisted the key and the door opened.

"Be careful," he said. "There's two steps down."

The old wooden steps creaked under Sam's weight. The ellipse of bluish light moved from Audie's legs to the doorway of the backroom.

"The books are in the back here," Sam said. "Unless she moved them." He stepped past Audie, tripped on the doorsill and stumbled into the dark room. "Damn it." The flashlight beam ricocheted around the book-filled walls.

"Are you alright?" Audie asked.

"Here they are," Sam said, bringing the light to two cardboard boxes. "Hold the light a minute." He handed the flashlight to Audie and went down on both knees to rummage inside the box with books in it. He found the little volume under the first book, where Alice had returned it. He left it there and turned to Audie. "These two boxes. Can you make two trips, kid? I got a bum knee and bum hip and every kind of bum bone you can name. Take that one first. I'll hold the door for you."

Audie returned the flashlight and bent to pick up the first box. "Heavy," he said, and stopped.

"What's the matter?" Sam asked.

"I thought I heard something. In the front."

"Cut it out, kid. You're making me nervous."

"Probably nothing."

After he had gone out the door, Sam turned the flashlight onto his white pants and brushed at the dirt on the knees. "What the devil!"

The noise had come from the front of the shop. A book had fallen to the floor.

Sam's heart bumped like something pounding to get out. The back door slammed behind Audie returning.

"Could you bring the light over here," Audie said. "I can't see anything."

Sam had his finger pressed to his lips to warn Audie, but he said aloud, "Kid, there's somebody ..."

A beam of light that seemed solid enough to sit on pinned him to the wall of books, moved toward him, and a voice pitched high with excitement said, "Stay where you are. You're under arrest. The both of you."

# THREE

Margaret Sawyer's car was too small for her. The top of her grey hair touched the cloth ceiling. The steering wheel when she turned it brushed the tops of her thighs. Otto Vandersteen pulled hard to shut the door on his side and when it was shut their shoulders touched. They looked like large children squeezed into a fairgrounds bumper car.

"Put your seatbelt on," Margaret said as she pulled away from the curb in front of Stubblefield's and up the steep hill. The taillights of Alma Ives' Cadillac had just disappeared over the crest.

Otto twisted and struggled with the buckle. The back of his hand touched Margaret's hip before the buckle clicked. "I hate these things," he said. He straightened himself and smoothed the top of his bald head. "I really could have walked, Margaret. It's not that far."

"I wanted to talk to you," Margaret said. She drove with one hand on the top of the steering wheel, the other in her lap. "I assume you're going on this excursion tomorrow, to Karlsson's place."

"No. I wasn't planning to. Really, Margaret, I've been there three times already. I don't see at all why I should go again."

"Well I do. If this collection is worth what Karlsson says it is, we can get a lot of good publicity out of it. I don't want another situation like the one with June Roth to develop. Karlsson could back out of this yet. He's a rather prickly fellow."

"He's a self-important ass. And June Roth is intolerable. I did everything I could to please her."

"Judging from how unpleased she appears to be, I would say you did not do a very good job, Otto. As usual." She shook her shoulders, gripped the wheel with both hands, and would have straightened up if the car's ceiling had allowed her to.

"If she had come to me in the first place, for my advice, instead of going to the Chancellor, for heaven's sakes, as if she were the Ford Foundation or some bloody thing, with a billion dollars to give, and then to you, who knows absolutely nothing about the problems of my department ..."

"You had no business shunting off half that collection to the stacks without consulting me. Good lord, Otto, he won the Nobel Prize."

"Do you seriously believe we could have devoted a whole room to his library? With his name in gold on the door and his portrait frowning down on us all forever? Out of that whole library there were less than fifty books that belonged in the Rare Book Department. That Robert Boyle collection of his, he was so fanatical about."

"Be that as it may, I want you to tell Sam Ives to be generous in the Roth appraisal. Perhaps we can placate June Roth a bit with a big tax deduction."

A small laugh, like a suppressed burp, sounded in Otto's narrow chest. "Well, I can't say that surprises me."

"What?"

"Don't you think that might be just the slightest bit unethical, for me to try to influence an appraisal?"

"What are you implying, Otto?" She stared at the side of his head long enough for the car to start drifting toward the curb, and she suddenly jerked it straight again, sending Otto's shoulder into the door frame and a road map sliding across the dashboard to the floor at his feet.

"Oh nothing," Otto said. "I imply nothing. It's just that, after the affair of the missing petty cash—which was really not so 'petty,' at least in my estimation—I would think that you ..."

Margaret's big hands squeezed the top of the steering wheel and the car began to go faster. She was silent for a minute, then said, "Is it you, Otto?"

"Me? What do you mean, Margaret?"

She hesitated again. "Gateway."

"Gateway? I have no idea what you are talking about."

She stared at him again, and Otto touched his forehead nervously.

"I'm warning you, Otto," Margaret said. "If it was you ..." She turned a corner sharply and this time Otto was pushed against her.

"Really, Margaret," he said, straightening himself, tugging at his trouser legs. "How ridiculous you sound at times. It's just the next block now, on the right."

"I know where you live."

"If you think it's so important, I will go along tomorrow. To Karlsson's 'island.' I have a ton to do, but, nonetheless ..."

"What was that exchange with Roger all about, when he asked you if anything had ever been stolen from Rare Books?"

"I have no idea. Just Roger being his obnoxious self."

"Could something be stolen from there?"

"I suppose it could. We take every precaution. Someone's always at the desk, watching the reading room. But even at the best universities ..."

Margaret swung to the curb in front of Otto's house and the little car's front wheel hit and climbed the curb and fell again. Otto braced himself against the dashboard.

"Sorry," Margaret said. "But Roger rather implied, didn't he, that someone could remove the catalog cards and any record that we owned a book, stealing it that way. That isn't possible, is it, with everything being online now? You should have told him that."

Otto's hand was on the door latch. "I would have told him that," he said, opening the door. "Except most of the rare books haven't been put online yet. You might recall my request for funds specifically for that last year. Good night, Margaret." He started to pull himself out of the car.

"Oh yes," she said, smiling at him. "We should do something about that, shouldn't we. Be obsequious as you can to Mr. Karlsson tomorrow."

"Good night." Otto tried to slam the door angrily but it didn't catch.

As she drove away, Margaret leaned across to pull it shut. "Little twerp," she said to herself.

ଔ

June Roth sat in her Toyota Camry until the others had pulled away. The street in front of Stubblefield's was so steep she felt as though she were leaning back in a recliner. She chewed at the only corner of fingernail she had left and watched the house windows. Stubblefield carried dishes from the dining room table to the kitchen. Roger must be in the kitchen. She snapped open the vinyl purse in her lap and reached in to feel the little gun she had bought last summer after one of the units in her condominium complex had been broken into. Do it, she urged herself silently. Now! They're such twits they'll admit it immediately. At least one of them will.

She opened the door carefully, as if afraid they might hear even in the house, and did not shut the door completely behind her. She clutched the purse with one arm against her breastless chest and stepped to the sidewalk, watching the windows. Without needing to, she went up on tiptoe. Alfred Stubblefield backed rapidly out of the kitchen door, flapping his arms as though doing a backstroke in water. She could hear his loud voice but not the words. He turned toward the living room and Roger came out of the kitchen shaking some instrument over his head and shouting.

June turned and hurried back into her car. What idiots, she thought. Ralph and Alice. It can't be them. She threw the purse angrily at the passenger door. The gun she had already forgotten clunked against the door. A passing car washed her windshield with headlights. She felt as if she had been caught window peeking, and started the car.

Everything was going so terribly wrong. What would Father think? His wonderful library. Well, she would not cry about it. She would make it right.

She drove on winding streets through College Heights and along the high street to a very large red brick house with a sloping, treeless lawn and a wide front porch on which she had sat many evenings with her father to watch the sunset across the campus, the lake just visible over the roofs of lower houses and tree tops further down the hill. She turned into the drive that lead along the side of the house to the single-stall garage, and put the car away.

On the first night after that terrible day when the plane had crashed, she had moved back home to live. She had put her condominium up for sale. She had always hated it, and had slept at "home" many nights after her mother had died. Why he would not let her move back permanently, take care of him, mind the house, she to this day did not understand. It had been her mother's idea she should have her own place. After all, you're a working girl now. You should have a place of your own, to entertain your friends, to decorate, to be "yours." They had even paid for it. The only good thing about it was she was able to have the birds. Her mother had only allowed her one pair at home. In the condominium the finches flew free, laid their eggs in coffee cups, perched on the lampshades, and only returned to their cages to eat and sleep. The most difficult thing about returning home (what furniture she had of her own remained in the condominium) had been moving the birds without harming them, for it had been late winter and she had had to wrap each cage in heavy covers and hurry to the heated car while the frantic birds fluttered inside.

She could hear them now as she unlocked the back door and entered the darkened kitchen: a commotion of miniature peeps and fluttering of tiny wings from the cages in the living room. She knew that when she turned the kitchen light on they would begin to leave their cages, and some would come to her and sit on her shoulder and even on her hair. She loved them so: their chunky, reddish orange beaks, the soft browns and grays of their feathers, the bright orange cheeks of the males, the gentle prick of their tiny claws.

Two fluttered over her, trying to land, as she went through the kitchen and into the living room. So as not to wake the other birds, she did not turn on the light. Ghosts of furniture loomed under the white sheets she had covered them with against the mess of the birds. She dropped her purse into the corner of the covered sofa, forgetting once again the gun, and went into the study.

The study was her refuge: her father's favorite room. Almost as big as the living room, it had its own fireplace. All the walls except the one with windows facing the street were lined with bookshelves. But the shelves were bare now. Against one case leaned the metal-framed Audubon plate of finches her father had given her for her birthday. She hadn't hung it yet. A large wooden desk stood in front of the windows, its sides carved with the busts of great scientists.

Who could it be, if not Alfred or Roger? she thought, and her narrow shoulders drooped as though the tiny weight of the birds perched now on each shoulder had become too much to bear.

The birds flew away as she dropped into the leather chair worn to the impression of her father's body. Above the fireplace her father watched her from the portrait the university had commissioned after he had won the Nobel

Prize: the kind eyes, the neat grey beard, the small smile, the pipe arrested half way to his mouth. On the end table next to her, the rack of pipes still stood in its accustomed place next to the tobacco humidor. She took one from the rack and filled it with the now dry tobacco. She brushed scattered strands of tobacco from the lap of her skirt. The pipe stem was white and scarred from his teeth. She put it in her mouth and lit it and drew down the match flame into the dry tobacco. The room filled once more with the dear smell of her father. She pulled her legs up under her and snuggled into the red leather of the chair as though into his arms.

"I'll make it right," she said aloud to the portrait. "I will. I promise. Don't ever worry."

At the sound of her voice, finches fluttered about her, seeming to hang onto the air with their moving wings before descending to land upon her in what she took to be an answer.

⍥

Clarence Biedermann saw his wife pass the living room window as he stood on the dark sidewalk under an old oak tree and watched that lighted world inside to which he belonged as unavoidably as tomorrow and the next day. She was wearing a pink sweatshirt and he thought of huge cotton candy. He knew the sweatshirt would proclaim in letters as large as her voice some passionate demand to free this or that, or save some creature down to its last few desperate specimens, or ban abortion. She returned and seemed to throw herself down suddenly under the window and he knew she had flopped onto the sofa she considered "hers" for watching television, two pillows propped under the disorder of her grey hair.

She had earned her PhD in German literature at Michigan the year before he had finished his own dissertation. They had married and, even without a position for herself, she had moved with him here when he was hired in the English Department. But after years of not being hired even as a semester replacement for someone on leave, she had become bitter, especially against the feminists, who she was convinced had conspired against her because of her pro-life views.

"I think if you would work on polishing your dissertation, dear," Clarence said. "If it were to be published, or at least chapters of it as papers, perhaps then ..."

"I know what it is, Clarence," she said. She had a way of tugging at the hair over her ear when she was excited that had at one time seemed charming to him. "And it's not my scholarship. You remember very well how Professor Andres praised the dissertation, and he was Norwegian, for heaven's sakes. No, it's they cannot tolerate a dissident voice. You'd think in a university community dissent views would be a virtue. What a laugh. Well, I will not be cowed."

She kept tacked to the bulletin board next to her desk in the study the whole front page of the State Journal featuring a colored photo of her leading a Right-to-Life march on the state capitol. She strode two feet ahead of the crowd in her sweatshirt and blue jeans, carrying a large sign like a cross on her shoulder.

Watching the house, he thought how totally he could change their life. He would not go up the worn wooden steps to the porch with the swing at the end; he would not pull open the screen door and hold it behind him while he fumbled with the brass doorknob that always stuck; he would not push the warped door open with his shoulder and pull it tight behind him; he would not ever again say "I'm home, dear."

"I'm home, dear," he said, bending to slip off the rubbers he had worn that morning when there had been the possibility of afternoon rain. She had heard him on the steps and was already coming through the wide archway to the living room. She waited until he stood and turned to her; then they embraced. He held her more tightly than usual for a moment (she must have had onions for supper) and said into her ear, invisible under massive hair, "I love you." But he wondered if he had said it aloud.

She started back toward the living room. "How was the dinner?" she asked, pulling down the hem of her sweatshirt. "Was Alfred bearable? Were there other women there? PBS is in one of its wretched fundraisers again. They've had this dreadful Swiss fellow chirping away for over an hour now. It's was awful, really. I could barely watch. And then they break away for fifteen minutes begging you to pledge them tons of money. Banks of people holding onto telephones like they're about to ring any second. You'll never guess who was there: Cora Cunningham, of all people. What a laugh."

He had only said it because he had suddenly realized when she had pressed against him that there was no one else in his life to whom he could say I love you. Certainly not Klaus, who lived upstairs in his room as though in another country, who exited through his computer screen into realms his parents could not imagine, who spoke in the tongue of technology. Taking him to Europe with him last semester had been Pearl's idea.

"We can't afford it, dear," he had said. "I couldn't go myself, without the grant money. Two extra people, three months ..."

"Just take him, then. I'll stay home. I'm used to that. Clarence, he's eighteen years old. He's never been out of the state, much less the country. Perhaps it's just what's needed. We'll talk to Doctor Boldt first, of course, and if he says it's alright ..."

The thought of sharing a room with his son for three months had been more than he could bear. Good lord, they might even have to share a bed at some point: those small hotels in Spain, with bathrooms down the hall. Perhaps it was that thought that had made him decide to use the grant money to pay for Klaus. Klaus Biedermann-Messer could become Klaus Messer, his research assistant. And he would be his assistant, too. It wasn't as if he were trying to cheat anyone. There were many things Klaus could do. Keep notes for him on his laptop, for one, while they were in archives and libraries. Perhaps he could even teach Klaus the methodologies of scholarship. It could be just the thing to start him thinking of a career. And he could have his own room. They would each have separate rooms. The grant money would pay.

"Was there any mail today, dear?" he asked.

"I put it on your desk."

"What was it?"

"Well, I don't look at your mail, Clarence. It's on your desk. Go see."

In his study he approached the disarrayed envelopes lying on top of a New York Review of Books as if there might be snakes. He pulled the heavy oak chair out from the desk and sat on its edge. He straightened the envelopes into a pile and with thumping heart began to tip them one at a time toward him. But there was not another envelop with his name, Professor Clarence Biedermann, typed on an old machine with a very faded ribbon; not another xerox of his travel expense report with the second airline ticket and Klaus Messer underlined in red felt pen; no more demands or instructions or reasons why. Still, he felt no relief. Water welled into his eyes and he put his shiny forehead down on the book review, tilting his glasses. A tear slid down the inside of the lens and he smelled it meld into the pulpy paper, but he did not lift his head.

Whatever would he do? But he knew what he would have to do.

# FOUR

Nick Ash looked at the woman across from him and wondered why he no longer felt anything for her, not even affection, much less physical attraction. She was still beautiful, but it was a hard beauty now, one that needed makeup, not to cover blemishes or creases, but to imitate warmth. Her tanned skin implied California sun and ocean beach but Nick guessed it had really come from the electric sun inside a machine. He knew she hated the outdoors. Their first night together he had rented a canoe from the student union's sailing club and paddled on the lake toward Picnic Point and she had been scared to death, holding to the sides of the canoe with white fists, and he had turned back before they were halfway there. So what if she didn't like to sail or swim or bike? She was twenty-one and gorgeous and he was ten years older and could think only of one thing.

"You look the same, Nick." She plucked the top of her very blond hair. "Maybe a little up here." She pushed a hand at him over the Margarita glass on the polished surface of the pedestal table between them. "I like it though. Makes you look even handsomer than I remember."

She glanced around the room. Over the long, curved bar an enormous stained-glass chandelier hovered like a gaudy space ship inspecting the bald bartender. Behind the bar, a huge mirror reflected three couples on high-back stools, and, along the mirror's bottom edge, multi-colored bottles of liquor. Crescent-shaped booths in beige leather lined the curved wall opposite the bar. Nick sat on a chair facing her in the booth, his back to the bar, a tumbler of Scotch on the table in front of him.

"This place looks the same, too," she said. "I used to think it was the most glamorous place on earth, you know. When you brought me here. Like a New York nightclub. The oak bar and everything. Marty told me it cost him two hundred thousand just to remodel when he bought it, and that was how many years ago. Looks like it could use some spiffing up again. Wonder where old Marty is now."

Nick took a drink of his Scotch and held the glass against his chin a minute, watching her as she studied her frosted drink in affected melancholy. He had backed out of being the one to tell her about Alice, had called Nielsen later in the afternoon and told him to send someone over there. Then she had called him at home in the early evening, saying she was so upset about Alice she just had to talk to someone. ("I don't know anybody in this town anymore, Nicki. Please?") So he had agreed to meet her at ten.

"I'm sorry about your sister, Claire," he said.

She looked up at him with the old flirtatious smile he remembered too well. "I changed my name, you know," she said. "It's Clarisse now, like Jodie Foster in Silence of the Lambs? Yeah, poor old Alice. It's really too creepy to think about. You might know it'd happen just when I'm back. Now I'll have to deal with the house and the store and the funeral and all that. It's a real mess, Nicki. I was planning on leaving in a few days. I have this audition lined up, you know."

"Why did you come back, Claire?"

"Oh, some business. Old time's sake."

"I've got Alice's dog. I was going to bring it over tomorrow."

"Gads, don't, Nicki. I've got enough to worry about besides a dog. Jeez." With a long red nail she began to flick the frost of salt off the edge of her Margarita glass. "Jeez."

That little pout of the lips he used to think was so sexy now irritated him. "Why'd you call me, Claire?

"Clarisse, Nicki. Come on, now." She pushed her hand at him playfully.

"I'll stick to Claire. Okay? We don't have time enough for me to get used to 'Clarisse.'"

"I don't know what to do about all this stuff, Nick. I mean the store and all. I don't know anybody here anymore, to help me. Except you. And I just wanted to see you again, too, you know, for old times' sake. See if you're still so handsome, you know."

"I'll keep the dog, if that'll help."

"I suppose it might be worth a lot of money." She was looking past his shoulder.

"The dog?"

"Gads, you can have the dog for free. I hate dogs. If you don't want it just put it down. Mangy old thing. You should see the dog hair all over everything. No, I mean the house. And the store. All those books and things. They're not even new books. I never could figure Alice, you know, Nick. I always figured she must've had different parents from me. Can you just see me running an old bookstore? Can you imagine that? And she was, like, at least twenty years older than me besides."

"Alice was damn good to you, Claire. Did she ever once turn you down all the times you wired you needed money or you'd lose your apartment or your car or some other great emergency?"

"She told you that? Well, gads Nick, you don't know how tough it is out there. There's tons of people looking to even get just a stupid commercial or something. You go there, like at six in the damn morning, and there's a line already. I hate to tell you all the stuff I went through out there. Hollywood. Boy. Anyways, Alice, she's supposed to help her kid sister. It's like a tradition of life, helping your kid sister. Right, Nick?"

"Whatever you say, Claire. Why're you so anxious to get back there, then, if it's so tough?"

"I just feel like I'm getting close, Nick. Something good is gonna happen and I gotta be there. You ever get that feeling, something good is gonna happen?"

"Not lately. So what do you want from me, Claire?"

"Nicki, I don't want anything. Why would you think that? Just old time's sake, is all."

Nick raised his glass. "Old times," he said.

Claire twisted her Margarita by the stem and dipped a red fingernail into the slush and touched her lip with the nail, leaving a sliver of ice there. "That cop guy that came this afternoon, Nick? He said they got Alice's body down at the morgue and I should come and identify her and 'claim her body' he says. Jeez, Nick. 'Claim her body.' Why would I want to claim her body?"

"You have to make funeral arrangements, Claire, when they release the body. Which may not be for a while, seeing she was murdered."

"Really? Like how long do you think?"

"How would I know, Claire?"

"Well, you're a cop, aren't you. I mean, a campus cop, but that's the same thing. Nicki, what do I know about 'funeral arrangements?' I never even saw a dead person, much less bury one. What I really have to find out is if Alice made out a will. I mean, there's nobody else but me in the family, so I'd be her, like they say, next of kin, right? But maybe she made out a will, anyways. How would I find out about that, Nick?"

Nick shrugged. "She'll have papers around someplace, I suppose. At home or in the store. You'll just have to look, find out who her lawyer was."

"Would you be able to do that, Nick? For me? I mean, I won't even be here. I could make you power of attorney, or whatever it is. You could see about selling the store, the house and stuff. I'd be willing to give you a cut."

"You're nuts, Claire. Look, it's almost eleven. I gotta go. Tomorrow's a work day."

She reached across the table and covered his hand holding the tumbler of Scotch. Her hand was very cold and her fingers felt like cold glass on the back of his hand and he almost pulled away.

"Don't go, Nicki. I mean, we haven't even talked about anything yet. Like about old times and stuff. Besides, I feel kind of scared, you know, with Alice killed, and all. How do I know the creep that killed her won't come to the house, looking for something? Come on, I'll buy you another one of those. Or we could go back to the house and have a drink there. You could 'secure the premises,' like they say. Do you still go swimming every morning, Nick, like you used to? In that gym pool. 'Member the time I surprised you there, that time I came to surprise you? Before we were ... you know. I used to think that was so sexy, Nicki, you swimming like that."

Nick leaned back in his chair and half laughed. "What the devil are you up to, Claire? What I remember is all the things you had to say when we broke up. That's what I remember."

"Aw, Nicki. There was so much going on then, what with Alice being mad at me and kicking me out, with me not having any money at all. And you wouldn't let me live with you. Don't forget that, Nicki. You don't know how hurt I was by you saying no that time. And me not getting any younger every day, with my dreams and all."

Nick laughed. "Man, you haven't changed one bit, have you, Claire. You must think I'm a real sap, I'd fall for your little games again."

Claire looked into her drink, tilting it around the edge of the glass. "Clarisse," she said, pouting.

"I've gotta go, 'Clarisse.'" Nick finished his drink and started to get up.

"I suppose you're still crazy over that Karen, Alice told me about," she said.

"Nice to see you again, 'Clarisse.'"

"Just wait a sec, Nicki. Sit down. Please? I'm scared. I'm not kidding, Nicki. I'm really kind of scared."

Nick's cell phone ringing startled them both. He pulled it out of his pocket. "Nick Ash," he said. He listened. Claire finished her drink in one swallow.

"Where are you now?" Nick said into the phone. "Well at least they didn't hold you." He laughed. "Alma can do anything. It's almost eleven, Sam. I suppose. I'm on Lake Street now. It's a long story. Look, I'll stop up. I'm walking, so it'll be twenty minutes, at least. Alright. Bye."

"Who's Alma?" Claire asked.

"I gotta go, Claire. Look, I don't want to be mean or anything, but there's nothing I can do to help you. I'll keep the dog for you, is about all."

She looked up at him standing, brushed her blond hair away from the side of her face, and moved her head a little to let the lights from the bar reflect in her forming tears. "Aw Nicki," she said.

"Bye, Claire."

"Sap," she called to his back.

ଓଷ

On the warm spring night students swarmed in front of the popular State Street bars like night insects attracted to neon. Nick had to walk in the street to get around them. The Brew Kup's outside tables were full. One young man sat on the sidewalk with his back against the wall under the coffee shop's plate glass window, a sleeping bag rolled up by his side, his bare legs stretched out on the concrete so people walking by had to step over them. A ferret with a miniature red collar was curled into a ball in his lap, sleeping.

He walked up Langdon Street, the smell of lake water noticeable now. Ahead, above the trees, he could see Langdon Manor and the lights of Sam's apartment on the top floor.

Alma answered the door. "Nick dear, you're an angel. I hope you can calm him down. He wants to sue the mayor now." She called over her shoulder, "Sam, Nick's here."

The big cat jumped down from Alma's chair and trotted to rub against Nick's ankles. Nick squatted and wrestled it to its back. "How's old Walt tonight?"

"He's in his office, Nick," Alma said. "Just go on in. I'm going to bed. I've had enough of him for today."

Nick hoisted the cat over his shoulder and it hung its head down, purring and kneading his shoulder blade with its claws. "Let's go see the old man, Walt."

Sam's book-lined office was at the end of a narrow hallway. He was standing behind a huge oak desk littered with books and papers. Copper lamps with amber mica shades stood on two corners of the desk. Behind him, two windows, close together, looked out on the lighted dome of the capitol building.

"Nick, Nick, I was arrested," he said, and plopped his heavy body into a green leather swivel chair. He reached for a tumbler of liquor and ice cubes sitting among papers on the edge of the desk. "First time in my life," he said after swallowing. "Not even in New York. Outrageous." The ice cubes clinked loudly in the shaking glass and he steadied it in his lap.

Nick dropped the cat to the floor. "What were you doing there anyway, Sam? You knew they had it taped off as a crime scene."

"Not the back door. There was nothing on the back door. We had a key. We weren't 'breaking and entering' anything, for gods' sakes. And I already paid for the books. I had a right to get my books, didn't I?"

"Who's we?"

"That kid Audie. He works there. He had a key to the back door and he said he'd let me in to get my books I already paid for. 'Breaking and entering,' bull. I don't think much of that friend of yours there, Nick. Nielsen. He even knows me, for gods' sakes. Acted like I was returning to 'the scene of the crime.' For gods' sakes. What's he think: I'm a murderer?"

"Did they charge you?"

Sam drank again. "Look at me still shaking," he said, holding up the trembling glass. "I'm so mad."

"Your hand's always shaking, Sam."

"Well, anyway." He stood and hooked his arm at Nick. "Nick, come around here and lift this up on the desk, will you. My back."

"What is it? Your famous books." Nick lifted the cardboard box and with its edge pushed papers aside on the desk. "What's so important you had to risk getting arrested? I'm surprised they let you take them."

Sam had lit a cigarette and exhaled a cloud of smoke at the ceiling. He laughed. "They didn't the second box, but I already had this one in the car, they didn't know about."

"Sam."

"Look, here's why I wanted you to come over." He picked up the small book bound in thick gray paper, creased somewhat. "Two things." He tapped the book's cover with a tobacco-stained finger. "This is a very important book, small as it is. *A Degradation of Gold*, Robert Boyle, 1678." He held the book open at the title page with his thumb and tapped it again. "Even though it doesn't say so here on the title page, it's by Robert Boyle. I know. One of his rarest. Only a few copies, four or five, left in the world." He held the book over to Nick leaning toward him. "Very rare. Worth a lot of money. All about alchemy and his fight with Newton."

"So? I thought it was this encyclopedia you were so hot about."

"This was in the box with the encyclopedia."

"That you bought from Alice."

"I bought the box of books, yes. She knew it was in there. She even showed it to me. I didn't know much about it at the time. Boyle's name's not on the title page. But I've got the ..." He reached for a book on his desk and hit its cover with his fist. "... the Boyle bibliography here, tells all about it. I had a hunch it might be, since I was looking at books by Boyle earlier this morning."

The cat jumped suddenly onto the desk and began walking across the scattered books and papers toward Nick. "Get out, Walt," Sam said, and pushed it. It slid off the desk, along with the papers it had been walking on. "Damn cat." Sam bent with a grunt to retrieve the papers. "Why're you looking at me like that, Nick? I paid Alice for the box of books, I told you."

"And she knew this 'Boyle' thing was in the box?"

"She knew. I mean, she didn't know how much it was worth, but I didn't either, at the time. Look, it was up to her to know how much what she's selling is worth. If I walk into a shop and find Poe's *Tamerlane* marked seventy-five cents in a box of old junk, I buy it. I don't tell the owner this is worth a fortune, moron. That's just how it works. Anyway, Nick, this is what I wanted to show you."

He pulled the cardboard box toward him across the desk. He bent over the box, squinted at the spines of the large green volumes, and pulled one out. "Come on around here and see this," he said. He thumped the heavy volume down on the desk and twisted his cigarette out in a metal ashtray on the rim of which a metal lizard crawled.

Nick moved the swivel chair out of the way and stood next to him. Sam tipped the book onto its front edges and tapped the spine.

"*Britannicas* were published in a lot of different formats," he said. "This is the thick paper edition, folio, but it's been issued two volumes in one. Not uncommon to do that. Alright, this is volume six and seven, Bar to Ced. Now look at this."

He laid the book flat on the desk and opened it. A space approximately ten inches square and an inch and a half deep had been carved out of the pages.

"You got robbed," Nick said.

"It's a hiding place," Sam said. He picked up the little volume of Boyle's *Of a Degradation of Gold* and set it into the opening. "Probably for this. It's the volume that would have the Boyle article in it: Bar to Ced."

"So?"

"So, I think the book was in there, like this, and whoever sold the encyclopedia to Alice didn't know it. Or else forgot it."

"You say it's worth a lot of money. How much, exactly?" Nick picked up the little book and turned the pages. "It's not even twenty pages."

"Well, it's not like a first edition of Copernicus, but if I were to sell it I'd probably ask fifteen thousand. I mean, Boyle and Newton on alchemy. Pretty exciting stuff."

"Fifteen thousand for this little thing? Well, if it's worth that much, it doesn't seem too likely someone would forget it was there and sell the encyclopedia when they were using it like some kind of safe. Who'd Alice get it from?"

"She wouldn't tell me. Audie—the kid that works for her?—said she came in just before closing last night with the encyclopedia and some boxes of paperbacks she said she'd just bought, but he didn't ask her from who."

He patted the cigarette pack in his shirt pocket and pulled it out. "You want a cigarette?" He held it out to Nick.

"Nope," Nick said. He picked up the big cat winding around his ankles and tucked it under his arm. "Walter, Walter. What about the other volumes? Are they cut up like that, too?"

"I didn't look." Sam shook the match away from his cigarette and dropped it in the ashtray. He pulled another volume out of the box on the desk. "I was interested in reading the article on Boyle, is why I looked at that volume. This one's alright." He lifted each volume out, opened it, and piled it on the others on the desk. One other had been hollowed out, but was empty. "Look's like just those two. At least in this box. I'm going to see that fellow Nielsen about the other box. He's got no right to keep my stuff." He dropped into his chair, took a deep pull on his cigarette, and reached for his drink. "What I'm thinking, Nick, is maybe all this has something to do with Alice's getting killed."

"How? I don't see somebody getting strangled over a book. Even if it is worth fifteen grand."

"Yeah. But what if there was something just as valuable in the other books. Like maybe there was something in this empty one."

"I think you should show this stuff to Nielsen. He doesn't even know you have it."

"Oh sure, and get arrested again. Not likely. Nick, I didn't even offer you a drink."

"No thanks. I had too much already. I've got to get going home, Sam."

"Where were you, when I called? I couldn't get you at home."

"I met a friend of mine at a bar."

"Who?"

"Just a friend. Former friend, anyway. Don't be so nosey, Sam. Down you go, Walt. I gotta go home."

"A woman? The one who called you last night? Alice's sister?"

"Yeah. She called me again."

"You still interested in her?"

"Not even a little bit. Mainly I went to see what she wanted to do about the dog."

"How'd she take Alice being killed?"

Nick shrugged. "Claire ... They never got along very well. Fought a lot. Claire's one of those people so wrapped up in themselves... I mean, she'd know when she went to bed what clothes she was going to wear in the morning. That'd be the last thing she'd think about in bed, how she was going to look the next day. You know what I mean?"

"What'd she want, then? That she called you."

"For old time's sake, she says. I suppose she's upset about Alice. What she really wants is for somebody to take care of burying her, sell everything she owned, and give her the money."

"Maybe she's not even the heir. Does she want to sell the bookstore, too?"

"I don't know anything about it, Sam. I could care less. I have to get home before that dog does something on the rug."

"Maybe I should talk to her about the books. I wouldn't mind buying some of the books. There's some reference things Alice had I ..."

"Up to you, Sam. She's staying at Alice's house. So, I'll see you tomorrow."

"Nick, we're going up to the Peninsula tomorrow, to see a book collection someone's giving the university. Why don't you come with?"

"I have to work."

"Well, it would be work. It's a valuable collection. The university should have someone from Protection and Security there, to figure out the best way to get it back here safe."

"I don't know. I'll talk to my boss about it."

"Call me first thing in the morning then. We'll probably leave around ten."

He walked home. He almost always walked. He liked to keep track of the number of days since he'd last taken his old Ford out of the falling-down garage that opened off an alleyway behind his apartment: something like fifteen days now. He took his bike more often than the car. On weekends in spring he would sometimes ride out as far as Fox Prairie, riding hard all the way, even up Springfield Hill, then swim in the river, lie in the sun on the river's sandy beach and watch the seagulls on the sandbars, people drifting down the wide river in innertubes or in canoes they'd rented at Hilverson's by the bridge in Fox Prairie. He'd get a milk shake at Dolly's Café, then ride back.

On State Street the crowds of students in front of the bars were more dense now, and more raucous. He walked in the street. As he passed Lowell's bookshop, a bus came up behind him and he had to move onto the sidewalk. The yellow crime-scene tape was stretched across the door.

At the corner he hesitated, looking down toward the Porta Bella, wondering if 'Clarisse' might still be there. If she was, she wouldn't be alone. Someone would have hit on her by now. He crossed the street to the library mall, almost deserted now the library was closed. A couple was kissing against one of the kiosks. They didn't look at him as he passed. At Park Street he decided to cross campus instead of going over to University, and he began to climb the steep sidewalk up the hill toward Bascom Hall. He could smell the waters of the nearby lake. Above him the new leaves of young maples seemed almost transparent in the globes of light atop concrete light posts lining the walkway. In the shadows to his left, century-old halls: Music, Law, Education, loomed like great ships, and to his right the broad, rolling lawn, rising in the moonlight up to Bascom Hall, could have been the silver sea.

He thought of Karen, as he always did on this steep sidewalk that drew him as inevitably as a compass needle north. He tried to shut his mind down against the song, but the unstoppable words came on a soundless melody: the first time ever I saw your face. And he saw her again as he did first, moving in the crowd a few feet ahead of him down the corridor in Music Hall after the intermission: her short blond hair, the green dress. Karen. Most of the people had stood in groups on the sidewalk, smoking, but she had gone out onto the lawn alone and sat, and after a while he had gone over and said hello. She was still a student then, but ...

I need a drink, he thought. Should've taken the one Sam offered. Maybe carry a flask. I'm a long way from home yet. They already think I'm a drunk. All I need is they find it in my pocket. Main thing is not to think of her being with someone else. Think of the dog. It's probably chewing the chair legs, pissing on the rug. The first time ever I saw your face.

And then the air turned black and only his body took him home because his mind was lost in the dark.

The dog saved him. He had stumbled twice climbing the three flights of stairs to his apartment in the old house: someone's mansion turned into flats, two to a floor except for his on the top. He had a hard time with the key in the lock. He went in and pushed the door shut with his back and stood in the dark a minute with his back against the door, feeling his heart pound. He switched on the light and the dog was sitting there, watching him. The dog didn't move, or wag its tail. The dog just waited.

"Well, look here," Nick said. "A dog. Imagine that." He went down on one knee next to the dog and pulled its head against his chest and flapped its ears. "What a good dog." He lifted the dog's head and the dog's tail began to wag. "Belle. You're my dog now. Okay?" The dog pushed its head against him. "Just you and me, old girl," Nick said. "Okay?"

# FIVE

Sounds of swimming echoed off the ceramic walls in heavy humid air that smelled as if it too had been chlorinated. Nick stood on the edge of the pool, swung his arms to loosen his shoulder muscles. Two swimmers churned the blue water in lanes at each side of the pool. Usually Nick was here first, but this morning he had had to walk the dog, after debating whether he could somehow bring it in to work with him. He curled his toes over the rim of the center lane, went up on the balls of his feet and down again, delaying the moment of shock that he both dreaded and looked forward to, when the cold water would rush over his body, scraping away like a shed skin a day and a night of accumulated life. He dove into a cleaner world, coasted under water, and rose to the surface, already set in his accustomed groove, arms pulling down strong through the water, face down then curled back over his shoulder, breath bubbling past his shoulder blade as if even his breath were water. He touched the tile wall at the end of the lane, somersaulted and kicked off.

He swam every day except Sunday, when the university pool didn't open until noon and then was too crowded. No matter how bad he felt from booze and cigarettes or the emptiness after Karen had left, he dove into cold water as if into confession, to emerge with a clean body reddened by the sting of chlorine.

He swam twenty laps. After the eighteenth, as he somersaulted away from the wall, he became aware of a figure standing at the end of his lane looking down into the pool. Why wait for his lane when there were plenty of empty ones? It looked like he was dressed, though. Nick came up against the wall after the twentieth lap and pulled his head up out of the water, sucking in air. No one was standing there. He pushed off the pool floor and pulled himself up onto the rim.

He went into the shower room first. There was no one there and he stood for a long time under the hot spray, arms folded, head down. Someone passed the arched entryway and he heard a locker open in the dressing room. He stripped off his swimsuit, rung it out and hung it on the shower faucet. The attendant hadn't put new soap into the metal trays yet, so he used the one sliver he could find to wash away the chlorine. He rinsed off, shut down the shower, and padded, dripping water, into the locker room.

The man was sitting on the long bench in front of an opened locker. He was still fully dressed and seemed to be studying intently something in the back of the locker.

Shit, Nick thought, the whole place is empty and he picks a locker right across from mine.

He walked carefully on wet feet on the thickly varnished floor to his locker. The man looked up as though surprised and nodded at him. Nick nodded, said "Morning", and bent, acutely aware of his nakedness, to spin the combination of his lock.

"Trying to get motivated here," the man said without getting up. "Hard to get started sometimes, so early, isn't it?"

"Feels good after, though," Nick said. He jerked open the sticking door of his locker and reached in for his towel. He threw it over his shoulder and tied his swimsuit to the vents on the inside of the door. He kept his back to the man as he dried himself with the towel.

"You swim every day?" the man asked.

Nick's head was under the towel as he rubbed his hair dry. "Try to," he said. He wrapped the towel around his waist and reached into the locker for his shorts.

Still sitting, the man turned toward Nick. He was wearing a forest green turtleneck and brown, wide-wale corduroys. He hugged a small vinyl gym bag in his lap, as if he were trying to keep something from jumping out.

"Well, I'm trying to get in the habit," he said. "I'm debating if I should swim or go up to the track and run some laps."

Nick didn't say anything. He dropped the towel and pulled on his shorts and reached in for his undershirt. He wiped his still bare feet standing on the towel.

"Where do you get towels around here?" the man asked.

"You should have got one before you came in the locker room," Nick said. "Where you showed your I.D."

"Oh. I didn't notice, I guess." He stood up then and held out a hand to Nick. "I'm Roger Limbert," he said. "I work in the Dean's office on the hill."

Nick pulled his undershirt down his body and took the man's hand. He was surprised how strong his grip was. "Nick Ash," he said. He reached into the locker again for his uniform shirt.

"I used to work out all the time when I lived in L.A.," the man said, watching Nick dress. "Here, with the winter and all, I just got out of the habit, I guess."

Nick buttoned his shirt without saying anything and started to pull on his pants.

"What kind of uniform is that?" Roger Limbert asked.

"Protection and Security," Nick said. He sat on the bench as far from Limbert as he could and bent to get his shoes out of the bottom of the locker.

"You work on campus then?"

"Yup." Nick dried a foot with the towel and pulled on a sock.

"I thought you looked familiar. I must've seen you around before. I work in the Dean's office on the hill."

"You said."

Other people were coming into the locker room now and there were sounds of conversation from other aisles and of lockers opening.

Roger Limbert stood. "Nick, to be honest with you, I already know who you are."

Nick looked up at him. "Look fella, if this is going where I think it is ..."

"I wanted to meet you because there's something I have to talk to you about. You think it would be possible to meet me for a drink sometime? Say this evening."

"Not a chance." Nick slipped on his shoes and bent to tie them.

"We have a mutual friend, you know."

"Yeah? Who's that?"

"Clarisse Lowell. You know Clarisse, don't you?"

Nick stood and they faced each other over the bench. "I know Claire, yes," Nick said, studying the other man's face now. "What's this about?"

"Meet me for that drink."

"I'm not meeting you anywhere. What the devil do you want?" The man seemed to have a smirk on his face. Nick slammed his locker door shut and clicked the lock.

"Clarisse's sister was killed yesterday," Roger said. "I'm sure you know that."

"So?"

"I need to talk to someone about that."

Nick threw the damp towel over his shoulder and combed his hair with his fingers. "Well I'm not your man. I can put you in touch with the city police, the detective in charge. Name's Nielsen."

"I'd rather talk with you." He smiled at Nick. "It's important."

"Talk to me here, then."

Roger looked over his shoulder as if someone might be listening. He frowned. "I can't here. Look, Nick, you know that bar at Park and Regent? Gino's? Meet me there. Say nine."

"Forget it." Nick started to walk away.

"Claire said ..."

Nick turned back to him. "Claire said what?"

Roger picked up his gym bag as if he were ready to walk out with Nick. "Look Nick, I really need to talk to you about this." He was frowning now.

"Damn it, about what?"

"Nine. Okay?"

"Shit." Nick walked away. He threw the wet towel into the laundry bin and leaned on the counter while the attendant reached for a clean one.

"There you go, man," the attendant said, handing him the towel.

He needed to go back to his locker to put the clean towel away, but he didn't want to run into Limbert again. He sat on a bench in an empty aisle and waited.

"What the hell was that all about?" he said aloud, and kicked the door of the locker in front of him.

03

Protection and Security two years ago had been moved into the old brick building that had once housed the university's Stores Department: a long, single-story building with rows of windows on each side and, at each end, entrances that opened onto the side streets it was built between. Next to it, Parking Lot 12 was already filled with multi-colored cars, all dutifully bearing the Lot 12 sticker on their rear side windows. Nick walked down the lot's blacktopped aisle toward two pigeons courting in struts and bobs. Morning sunlight flashed off the windshields of the parked cars. Today'll be the first hot day, Nick thought. He tugged at the front of his shirt. He had started to sweat in the walk from the university gym. The pigeons hurried on orange feet to one side as Nick passed, but did not fly.

Inside the building there were no walls between the metal desks arranged at various angles at the far end of the long room. In the corner near the desks a cubicle with half-glass sides and no ceiling had been built for the department chief. Rows of florescent lights under metal shades hung from the ceiling on long rods. Among the desks stood empty coat racks and occasional mesh-caged fans on poles. Outside the chief's office a woman in her fifties, wearing a pink blouse, was studying a computer monitor, but the rest of the desks were empty.

Nick crossed the empty end of the room toward his desk. The floor was coated with the same heavy varnish as on the gym floor. He pulled out the rolling chair. A desk light was on in the chief's office, but he could not see if she was at her desk.

"Oh Nick," the woman said, suddenly aware of him. "You had calls already. A Mr. Ives called earlier and Detective Nielsen. I left the numbers on your desk there."

"Okay, thanks. Is the chief in?"

"Right behind you," she said, coming from the restroom.

"Got a second?"

"Come on in. Your hair's wet."

"I was swimming." He followed her into the imitation office, smiling to himself that she had noticed his hair.

Rose Delaney wore the same khaki uniform that the five men and the two other women in the department wore, even though, as chief, she would not have had to. She was young and pretty and Nick knew she looked great in a dress and most of the men wished she would wear one, or at least slacks and a blouse. Nick thought he knew why she dressed in uniform but he never mentioned it to her. They had gotten off to a bad start three years ago when the university brought her in to be Chief of Protection and Security after Max Leonard had dropped dead one day eating his lunch at his desk, spilled Coca-Cola running into a waxed bag of French fries. A bad start not because she was a woman—he rather liked that idea—but because he was still close to bottom in that mud-hole depression Karen had pushed him into. So when he did

"No. How would I see it? You know where it is in here? Show it to me."

Nick hesitated. "Well, it's in two boxes. Cardboard boxes. He got one of them last night. The other one's probably in the back yet."

"He got one. You mean he took something out of here?"

"Al, the guy's a book nut. You know how they are."

"Nut is right. Can't wait to read an encyclopedia, for gods' sake. Where the hell is this box?" He started down the aisle toward the back room and the young cop squeezed himself against the shelves to let him pass.

"Morning," Nick said to the young cop, turning sideways to pass him.

"These ones here?" Nielsen asked. He pointed at the box of green volumes on the wooden floor of the narrow room.

"Look, Al, I should tell you," Nick said. "Sam called me last night after he got back to his place, from talking to you. Wanted me to come over. He gets himself so worked up sometimes. Anyway, he showed me the books, and the thing is, some of them were hollowed out–well, one anyway–a square cut out of the center of the pages, so you could use it to put things in but it would still look like an ordinary book on the shelf."

"That right?" Nielsen went down on one knee on the dirty floor, pulled one of the heavy volumes from the box, and opened it. "This one's alright." He pulled out another and opened it onto a hollow center. "Like this you mean?" He held the book up to Nick. "Just a slip of paper. Noting worth hiding."

The paper had been torn from a notebook, the holes along its edge ripped and ragged.

"List of something," Nielsen said.

Nick took the paper. In red ballpoint someone had written:

Plate 1 Wild Turkey

Plate 53 Painted Finches
Plate 391 Wood Duck
Plate 376 Canada Goose

"I'll keep that," Nielsen said, taking the sheet back. "What's the story on the books? According to your buddy Mark Twain."

"Sam had bought the books that morning, yesterday, just before Alice was killed. He must have been close to the last one to see her."

"So he told me. And this Alice had bought the books the night before, from somebody she wouldn't say who. You think they might have something to do with her getting killed?"

"I don't know, Al. Seems a little farfetched to me. Makes more sense it was somebody came in off the street, like you thought in the first place. What about the cash register? Was there money missing?"

"There wasn't much money in it, but she had a bunch of cash in her purse, that was sitting under the desk. She probably got killed before she had time to load the register. Well, I'll get Conway to get what prints he can off the books. The way they've been handled, they're probably no good to us. I want that box your friend's got. Fact, I'll go get it now. Crazy bastard. I could charge him. I would have last night if he hadn't had his wife with him, and that kid. Where's he live, you know?"

"Langdon Manor. But I don't think he's there now. I called a while ago."

Nielsen looked at his watch. "Well, I'm outta here."

He turned and started down the aisle of books and the young cop hurried in front of him as though in danger of being run down. Out on the sunlit sidewalk he turned to Nick. "Alright, I'll see you then. You're looking good, Nick. Everything okay?"

"Yeah, great."

"Still like the job?"

"Sure. It's great. No pressure. Boss is a lot better looking than you ever were."

"That right? So, you like guys now?"

Nick laughed. "She's a woman."

"What next? What'd you do with that dog?"

"I'm keeping her."

"Good. That's good, Nick. Always thought you should have a dog. Keeps a guy from talking to the booze. See ya, Nick."

The squad car made a slow turn on the sidewalk, waited for a bus to pass on State Street, then bounced down the curb, its bumper scraping concrete. Across the street, the big clock in the window of Holder's Optical read nine-fifteen. Nick started up toward the Brew Kup, thinking he might find Sam there.

Sam Ives sat in the sunlight that poured through the bay window of the Brew Kup, the New York Times held up close to his face as if he were reading a road map. Nick followed two girl students through the door, stepped behind Sam, and flicked his ear.

"Nicolas," Sam said. He pushed up in his chair and folded the paper. "I called you earlier. Sit down." He grabbed his briefcase from the other chair and put it at his feet. He was wearing his white seersucker suit and red tie. His eyes were bloodshot and his plump cheeks sagged like leaking balloons. "You want some coffee?"

Nick sat and looked back at the counter. "Too long a line."

"Get one of those cups and I'll give you part of this. I just got it. I've had too much anyway."

When Nick brought the cup back Sam poured the coffee with trembling hand. "Are you coming with us, then?" he asked.

"With you? Oh, to the Peninsula. No, I've got to stick around here. You'll be gone all day. You don't look so hot, Sam."

"Didn't sleep. Thanks to being arrested like a common thief."

Nick laughed. "You're lucky they didn't charge you with something. I just saw Nielsen down at the bookstore and he wants the other box of books you've got."

"You told him?"

"I had to, Sam. You should never have taken it out of there. I didn't say anything about that book about gold that was in there. You should turn that over, too, though."

"What he doesn't know won't hurt him. As my grandmother used to say. Has he got the rest of the books?"

"He's having them fingerprinted. They might have something to do with Alice getting killed, Sam. You said so yourself, last night."

"Was there anything in the other volumes?"

"No. There was a slip of paper in the bottom of one of them with a list of stuff on it."

"What kind of stuff?"

"Birds of different kinds."

"Birds? Hmm." He looked up at his bushy eyebrows.

"Sam, you know somebody in the Dean's office name of Limbert? Roger Limbert?"

"Roger Limbert? That's Stubbblefield's partner, 'significant other.' We were just there for dinner last night. What about him?"

"I was at the pool this morning, he made a point of meeting me. Wants me to meet him for a drink tonight to ..."

"My, my Nick. You do attract everyone, don't you."

"It's not that. The thing is, he knows Alice's sister, Claire."

"Ah, another of your admirers. You amaze me, Nick."

"He made it sound serious. Like it might have something to do with Alice getting killed."

"How does he know Claire? You said she lives in California now."

"Apparently he did too, at one time."

"Are you going to meet him?"

"Don't know. I told him no. What do you know about him?"

"Only that he's Stubblefield's partner. Rather a prickly fellow. It seemed liked he was on the verge of arguments with just about everyone last night."

"Who's this Stubblefield?"

"English professor. He works with Alma."

"You know how long they've been together? Roger and him."

"Well, no, actually. We were there for dinner a couple times last year and he was there. Did the cooking. So over a year anyway." Sam gathered his newspaper and reached below the table for his briefcase. "Nick, I've got to get going. I'm suppose to meet at ten for this trip up north. Sure you won't come?"

Nick stood. "No. I've got to go home at noon to let that dog out."

Sam laughed. "Nick, Nick, so domesticated."

# SIX

Lars Karlsson leaned over the steering wheel and adjusted the rearview mirror so by tilting his head slightly he could see Audie sitting in the corner of the back seat.

"Just remember I can see you two back there," he said.

"I'll scream if he tries anything, Dad," Karla said from her corner. She grinned at Audie, but he kept looking out the window. "I think he's still scared from having been arrested last night, though."

"I wasn't arrested," Audie said. "They just asked me some questions and let me go."

"You led that boy astray, Sam," Karlsson said.

They had left the last suburb and were on the divided highway north to the Peninsula. Sam, sunk deep in the soft leather of the front seat, grunted and reached under his suit coat to touch the pack of cigarettes in his shirt pocket. The Cadillac's interior smelled of cigars, but Karla had insisted that neither Sam nor her father smoke.

The highway skirted small towns that seemed to have been dropped from the sky to block unsuccessfully the road's path, then ran north through the flat central counties that ages ago had been covered first by a vast ice sheet and, after the ice melted, an even greater lake. Now an immense chain of marshes, linked by meandering streams, stretched across the better part of two counties. North-migrating flocks of Canada geese as big and noisy as moving armies swarmed downward on banked wings to raucous argument with rafts of coot, mallards, teal, mergansers, and fellow geese drifting in ponds of open water among the winter-dried reeds and cattails. Farmers had plowed for planting the cornfields that edged the marsh, and crowds of geese strutted the rows for what they could find in the newly turned earth.

Karlsson leaned as far forward as he could over the steering wheel to watch a band of geese descend across the highway. "They'd better not crap on the car," he said.

"Dad, they're beautiful," Karla said from the back seat. "It's amazing."

"I never saw so many geese," Audie said. "I don't think they have geese in California."

"In another couple weeks they'll all be gone," Sam said. "Most of them anyway. Further north to the lakes."

"You ever been up to the Peninsula before, Sam?" Karlsson asked. He tilted his big chin up as though he were blowing cigar smoke at the car roof.

"Certainly," Sam said. "Several times. We rent two weeks in the fall from one of my wife's colleagues who has a place on the shore."

"Which shore? Lake or bay?"

"The lake side. I prefer it. The water's colder for swimming, but it's not so crowded. I can't take those cute tourists towns on the bay side very long."

Karla leaned forward to the back of the seat between them. "Oh, but I think they're charming, Mr. Ives. Like New England towns."

Sam only grunted.

"You're going to love it, Audie." Karla sat back and touched Audie's shoulder. "The island, especially. Wait 'til you see."

"You've never been to the island, though," Karlsson said. "Private island, but it's not far enough off shore. Damn rowboats can reach it even, if the water's not rough. I pay two guys to guard the place, what with all the stuff the old man stashed there. So, Sam, what do you think? Can you appraise this for me today?"

"Today. Not a chance. The best I can do today is look it over. If the collection's as big as you say, I'm going to need first of all a list of everything. Did your grandfather have it cataloged?"

"Cataloged? Shi... Shoot, I don't know. He was always monkeying around with it. Spent more time on those damn books than he did the business, the last years." Karlsson suddenly shouted at the ceiling. "Honey, did Grandpa make a list of those books?"

"Yes," Karla said. She sat watching the passing country, her freckled arms folded over the university logo on her red T-shirt. "There's a file cabinet there, a card cabinet with all the books on cards, like they used to have in libraries."

Sam turned sideways to look back at her. "What about correspondence? Did he keep his correspondence with book dealers?"

"Well, I don't know about that. Probably he did. He kept everything. Anyway, I remember when he would get books, lots of times I was there and he would unwrap them to show me, and I remember he would make cards for them and write down how much he paid and who he bought them from."

"Never paid any attention to him and those books," Karlsson said. "Anyway, there's your answer. That should help, right? Having a catalog with prices, like that. Shoot, maybe I don't even need you. You look expensive."

"Indeed. The prices will be out of date, of course, but it will be helpful, nonetheless. I'll have to have the catalog brought to my apartment."

"We'll bring it back with us today," Karlsson said.

"Dad, it's drawers and drawers."

"So? I've got a big trunk. What else you need, Sam?"

"The correspondence will be helpful."

"You've got it. You understand I want this wrapped up as soon as possible. And the books out of there. Anything else the library wants. I wanna put the place up for sale this summer yet, if possible."

"Daddy, I hate you." Karla reached to slap him on the back of his head. "You can't sell it. It's my house. Grandpa always said it was mine."

"Sure he did." Karsson grinned at Sam. "You got kids, Sam?"

"Not at the moment," Sam said. He cracked the window a bit and the roar of outside wind rushed in.

"Whoa," Karlsson said, reaching for the dashboard. "Shut that. I'll turn on the air conditioner, you're hot."

"It's stuffy in here," Sam said, and shut the window.

During the remaining two hour drive, the landscape became increasingly dominated by fields of dairy cows, red barns alongside white farmhouses, and, after they left the divided highway, occasional cheese factories that hugged the very edge of the county road. Sam, drowsy, listened to Karlsson tell the Horatio-Alger history of his grandfather, the immigrant boy who read every book he could find–his physics textbook over and over again–and, when he wasn't reading, tinkered with the parts of things until he understood how they worked. At seventeen he had left the farm for Chicago to work in one of Edison's plants and at night diagramed on sheets of scrap paper machines he saw already assembled in his mind. He dreamed more often of coils and armatures, of dynamos and electromagnets than he did the bodies of women. He invented an ignition device that he eventually sold to Ford and then built his own factory to manufacture it. With a fortune to spend, he began to buy rare books.

"How he ever got bit by that bug I don't know," Karlsson said. "My grandmother claimed he spent more money on those dumb books than he did on the house. They lived in just this ordinary white frame house in Chicago. He even kept the books in his office, the house was so small. Then he went up to the Peninsula one summer on vacation–I was along, according to my mother, but I don't remember–and of course he had to go to the very tip and he saw that rocky island out there off the end and he made up his mind right then to buy it and build this estate there. God only knows how much he spent. Had to haul all the building materials in on boats, all that rock he used. Hired half the population of the Peninsula at the time to work for him. Queer old bird he was. Never liked me especially, or my father. I don't think he even liked his wife as much as he did those books of his."

"He liked me," Karla said from the back. "I was his favorite."

"You were too little not to like," Karlsson said. "Besides, he was senile by then. Probably thought you were some kind of toy."

"You run the factory now?" Sam asked.

"Have for years. My father died before the old man did. Heart attack. So now I'm stuck with this unusable house on an island and a bunch of old books. I'll sell the house and the island and I'll give the books to the state for a tax deduction."

"He's really giving the house to me, Mr. Ives," Karla said. "He just doesn't know it yet."

"You're going to pay the taxes? The upkeep? Don't make me laugh."

"Audie," Karla sang softly. "Audie's sleeping." She laughed and poked his shoulder, but the sleeping boy, slouched against the door, head back and mouth open a little, didn't move.

"Little crook had a busy night," Karlsson said. He ducked his head to look in the rearview mirror. "Getting arrested."

"The condition of the books will make a big difference," Sam said, "as to their value. Are they on shelves? I hope they're not packed away in boxes."

"They're in the great hall, what the old man called the 'great hall,' in bookcases with glass doors. This house is built right on the shore of the island, out of rock, and there's a boat launch built below it, so you can drive a good sized boat in and dock it and climb the stairs into the house."

"That doesn't sound ideal conditions for books," Sam said.

He was watching the passing landscape and beginning to feel sleepy again. The flat, open pastures had begun to show eruptions of rock now, huge, tilted planes of reddish rock that protruded from the grassy fields as if they had been dive-bombed into the ground. Stands of dark green cedars slashed by white birches separated the fields. Potholes of water edged with marsh grass and cattails appeared. Redwing blackbirds flocked to these placid ponds and ducks and other waterfowl floated there to rest before encountering the wilder waters of the bay or the great lake. They entered the first town at the base of the Peninsula, the county highway leading straight into the main street to the stop light at the crossroads in the town's center.

"There's a big shipyard here," Karlsson said. "Out on the edge of the bay. They make a lot of ships for the government."

Sam had been here before and felt annoyed as Karlsson continued to talk like a tour guide. He needed coffee and a cigarette and, most of all, to get out of the car: a confinement he had never been able to endure for longer than a taxi ride.

"I've eaten at that café on the corner," Sam said. "They have very good pie. We could stop for a break."

"No way," Karlsson said. "The others are probably there already."

Once out of town again, Audie, who had woken at the stoplight, suddenly shouted right behind Sam's head, "There's the lake! Man, its looks as big as the ocean."

The road had been hemmed in by a cedar forest but as they crossed a bridge over a small stream the lake became visible quite close to them, its vast blue stretching to the horizon and a sky of the same blue. A tiny ship seemed painted on that blue wall.

There was not what could be called a town at the tip of the Peninsula where the others waited, only a haphazard accumulation of buildings, most of them separated by sandy fields: a weathered grocery store with white paint curling off grey boards and a big front window lettered in arches, Curtis Bogner Grocery; a concrete block gas station painted bright blue, with a rusted pickup truck parked next to its one pump; a tavern converted from the first floor of what had once been a two story house. The few houses built along the shoreline seemed to be leaning away from the wind that blew whitecaps crashing onto the sand. There were no trees.

"Get rid of all this crap," Karlsson said holding up an arm as if to present something. "I always figured this'd be a great place for one of those super resorts: big hotel, golf course, tennis courts, all that. Given the view from here. Great beach. Problem is the winters here are something else. Last half the year. And the rest of the time the wind blows like crazy."

He pulled the Cadillac up next to a white van parked at the end of a pier alongside of which what looked like a tugboat bobbed on the waves. The van was on Sam's side and from its windows the expressionless faces of Clarence Biedermann behind the wheel and Otto Vandersteen in the back looked down at him as if they had been imprisoned there for years and never expected to be freed. Karla and Audie were already getting out of the car. On the pier a small black dog had jumped off the boat and came barking toward them. A stout man in Bermuda shorts emerged from the boat's cabin and crossed his arms, waiting.

"Here we be," Karlsson said, rolling out of the car.

The wind pulled the car door away from Sam as he swung his legs out. Still sitting on the seat, he lit a cigarette, and held onto his flying hair.

Alfred Stubblefield, struggling to zip the front of a flimsy red windbreaker over his big stomach, came around the front of the van. "We've been waiting here for ages," he said. A scowl converged ridges of flesh onto the upper rims of his glasses. "I'm terribly worried about the waves." He turned back as if to see whether the waves were still there. "I don't really think we should attempt this. It was much less windy when I was here last."

"Nonsense," Karlsson said, already striding past him toward the pier. "Elmer's all set for us." He waved at the man on the tugboat. Reluctantly, Stubblefield followed him.

The air smelled of wet sand and seaweed, beached clams and fish. Over the bobbing tugboat a raucous crowd of seagulls balanced on the wind, as though waiting for the trip to begin. Out above rows of whitecaps the island rose like a rock castle in the sunlight.

"Can you see the house?" Karla said to Audie. They were standing in front of the Cadillac and the wind pressed their clothes against them. She pointed toward the island, then turned and threw both arms around Audie and hugged him. "Isn't it beautiful? I told you."

"It's like the ocean," Audie said. Karla started after her father. Audie looked down at his flapping t-shirt and said, "I should've brought a jacket."

Biedermann and Vandersteen climbed down from the van and stayed behind its doors for protection from the wind. Biedermann wore a maroon beret and a heavy wool sweater he had bought in a duty-free shop at Heathrow. He looked like a stout French farmer just come apprehensively into Paris. Otto Vandersteen's London Fog was belted tightly at his narrow waist. With one hand he protected the shining skin of his bald head.

"This is a very bad idea," Biedermann said. "I see no earthly reason for my having to be here. Margaret ... well, never mind, never mind."

"Where have you people been?" Vandersteen demanded of Sam. "Sitting over coffee, no doubt. Get out of here, dog." He pushed a leg at the little dog attempting to sniff his wingtips.

Sam remained sitting sideways, legs out of the car, smoking. He grinned at the two. "This is going to be more interesting than I thought," he said.

Sam dropped his cigarette butt to the sandy gravel and crushed it with his foot. "We'd better get to the boat," he said, standing. Alongside the boat Karlsson was waving both arms over his head at them.

Car doors slammed and the little dog raced ahead of the men. Biedermann held down his beret with one hand and covered his mouth and nose with the other, as if the wind were full of sand. Vandersteen plunged both hands deep into the pockets of his trench coat and walked with his bald head down to butt the wind. Sam's red tie had been immediately blown over his shoulder and the tails of his seersucker sport coat flapped like white wings at his sides. As they neared the pier the grassy sand gave way to beach sand that shifted under their shoes. On the bobbing boat the others waited, Karla holding to Audie's bare arm, Audie with his shoulders hunched and hands deep in the pockets of his shorts.

At the rear of the boat bluish bubbles of exhaust broke out of the rough water. Screeching seagulls dropped and rose over the boat. The stout man climbed off the boat onto the pier and in turn took each of the men by the arm to hand them like refugees into the boat. Stubblefield and Vandersteen went immediately into the cabin.

"See what I mean by wind?" Karlsson shouted at Sam. "It's not always this bad though."

The stout man had unloosed the boat from the pier, jumped in again, and hurried into the cabin, followed by his dog. Through the grimy windows Sam saw him move the others out of his way.

"That's Elmer Stroud," Karlsson said. "One of the natives. His grandfather helped build the place out there. He's made this trip a thousand times."

As the little boat swung into the wind and headed toward the island, Karla and Audie moved to the prow to sit against the front of the cabin and watch the seagulls and the breaking whitecaps. Karlsson and Sam, to be out of the wind, leaned against the cabin on each side of the door. Sam locked his knees and pushed back on the wall to brace himself against the boat's roll and bounce.

"Give me Chicago any day," Karlsson shouted at him. "I hate nature."

Away from land the waves seemed rougher, but the boat was moving faster now and able to plow through most of them, sending spray swishing past the corners of the cabin. Two and three at a time the seagulls began to leave for the retreating shoreline. Karla and Audie, hugging themselves with wet arms, moved from the prow and squeezed into the cabin with Vandersteen, Stubblefield, and Biedermann. The prow rose suddenly on a higher wave that rolled foam-flecked along the boat on both sides. The boat's bottom thumped the water hard and Sam's knees buckled so he had to grab the doorframe. Inside the cabin all but the captain at the wheel bounced into each other.

After ten minutes Sam was beginning to think he might get sick when suddenly, in the protection of the island, the wind died. Both men straightened away from the doorframe and brushed at their clothes. Sam discovered his tie was over his shoulder and pulled it back in place. The others came out of the cabin and stood at the rails as Elmer Stroud guided the little boat chugging through calm water toward a massive stone house set amid towering Norway pines on the island's shore. A high wall of mortared rocks rose to meet a steeply sloped roof of grey slate. Tall arched windows were spaced evenly across the wall of the house. A deck on massive pilings fronted the lower part of the building, and below the deck two arched openings, like caves at the foot of a cliff, allowed the water under the building. As the boat approached, swallows swirled out from under the deck to scatter along the island's shore.

The boat entered under the house, the putt-putt of the motor echoing off the damp walls. Stroud cut the engine and let the boat slide to the long walkway from which a row of old tires hung to protect the boat's side from rubbing concrete slick with green algae. Suddenly he hurried out of the cabin, knocking aside Stubblefield, and jumped onto the pier to secure the boat.

Karlsson and Audie climbed out of the boat and turned to help the others onto the walkway.

"I'd hoped never to come here again," Biedermann said. He held his hands folded against his lips as if in prayer. He looked around the boathouse dimly lit by a row of grimy light bulbs encased in cobwebbed cages along the wall. "It's medieval, in the worst sense."

"It's so Edgar Allen Poe," Stubblefield said, chuckling. "I love it. One expects a skeleton chained to the wall."

Sam cupped his hands around the cigarette he was lighting. He tossed the match into the oily water and drew smoke in deeply. It was only then he realized he had left his briefcase in the car. "Damn," he muttered.

Karlsson jogged up the steps at the end of the walkway. Audie and Karla followed him.

"I hope there are writing materials here," Sam said to Biedermann as they walked toward the stairs. "I left my briefcase in the car."

"I wish you had left me in the car," Biedermann said. He looked up at Sam with eyes that seemed tear filled. Under his badly trimmed Hemingway beard, his sad little mouth stirred like a mouse trying to hide. His beret, which in the wind he had pulled down too tightly onto his white hair, looked more like a woman's cap than the subtle reminder of the literary life he had intended.

"Are you alright, Clarence?" Sam asked. "You look rather bad."

"I see no reason on earth I should be here," he said. "I should never have let your wife talk me into this ridiculous Friends of the Library business. I was supposed to be only a figurehead. Margaret Sawyer is an absolute harridan, insisting I accompany this oaf Karlsson all day like a pet dog."

"Well, it is an important book collection, from the sound of it," Sam said.

Biedermann had stopped at the foot of the stairs and put a hand to his eyebrows. "Just now, when I have so much on my mind."

Sam, already two steps up, looked unavoidably at the broad rear of Alfred Stubblefield laboriously climbing the steps. He did not see Biedermann pull out the red bandana he used in place of a handkerchief and stop to weep. When Sam reached the landing at the top of the long stairway, he could feel his heart pounding. Through an arched doorway he saw the others in a group looking up and when he entered to join them, Karlsson raised his arms to the high ceiling as if he were some kind of celebrant.

"The Great Hall," he said in capital letters. "When I was a kid this place scared the hell out of me. I thought it was the dungeon where they kept the Count of Monte Cristo."

"And I always thought it was a castle," Karla said. "A castle on an island in the sea."

The hall had a high, pitched ceiling and walls made of the same rock as the exterior. Heavy beams crossed from wall to wall at the tops of the tall windows. Below the windows both of the long sidewalls were lined with metal book cases with glass doors barred diagonally by metal strips. Long tables and cabinets were arranged at various places around the room. At the far end leather chairs and a large desk fronted an enormous rock fireplace with a mantel made from the peeled trunk of an ancient pine. Lamps constructed of deer antlers stood on all the tables and cabinets, and in front of the fireplace a Polar bear skin with snarling head lay like a patch of dirty snow.

"So, what do you think, Sam?" Karlsson said. "Impressed?"

"I think your grandfather must've been dropped off by the Vikings."

Karlsson laughed loudly, startling two sparrows that fluttered chirping about the beams, trying to find where they had gotten in.

"Well, I have to sit down," Otto Vandersteen said, "if you're going to give tours." He crossed to one of the long tables, pulled out a high-backed chair and sat as stiffly as the chair back itself.

"I'm showing Audie the island," Karla said. She pulled Audie by his arm toward the door where Biedermann stood as though waiting be invited in.

"I'll give you a tour if you want," Karlssson said to Sam. "The living quarters are off the wing at the end of the room there. Hell, we don't have time for a tour. The books are all in here. You can just get started. What about the furnishings? Can you appraise those, too? I want to get rid of everything."

"Not my line," Sam said. He walked toward the bookcases. "Are these locked? Where are those files–the catalog–you were talking about?" He looked up at the ceiling where the sparrows still flew from beam to beam. "This is a hell of place to keep rare books."

"I know where the keys are," Stubblefield said. "In the desk. There are magnificent things here, Sam. Wait until you see. The Audubon folios are here, in this case." He ran a finger over the dusty surface of a large desk-like cabinet with shelves below. "Have you ever seen the elephant folios?"

"Good lord, Alfred," Otto Vandersteen barked. "He's not going to have time to look at everything. Especially the Audubons. It would take both of us to lift them out of there."

"Yes, I suppose you're right," Stubblefield said. "Well, there's plenty to see. I'll just get the keys."

The warning tone in Vandersteen's voice made Sam curious. Supporting himself with one hand on the cabinet, he leaned to look at the spines of the enormous volumes shelved horizontally there. "Are they in full leather?" he said. "I've never seen full leather on anything so big."

"Here are the keys," Stubblefield said, hurrying back. He seemed always to be walking on tiptoe when he hurried. "I've never been able to figure out the order of things here, so let's just start anywhere." He held a ring of small keys up and began to fumble through them.

Karlsson said, "I've got to check on the rest of the place, talk to the watchman." He looked at his watch. "How long you think this'll take?"

"I just need to get an idea of what's here, what kind of condition the books are in," Sam said.

He turned to Clarence Biedermann, who was standing forlornly beside Otto Vandersteen's chair. He had taken off his beret and was circling the rim with trembling fingers, as though saying a rosary.

"Maybe one of you could pack up the files and the catalog," Sam said. "If you know where they are." Neither of them seemed to have heard him.

Stubblefield shook the metal door of the first bookcase as he twisted a tiny key in the lock. "These locks stick terribly sometimes," he said as he pulled open the door. "I'll just dart on ahead and open the others for you, Sam."

The metal bookcases were ugly. Even the shelves were metal. Sam thought old man Karlsson must have hauled them into his office from someplace else in the factory, where they would have been used to store things less elegant than books. But the books were elegant. Even Sam was stunned. The case was crammed with small octavos, most of them bound in full morocco of various shades of crimson and green, the spines and covers skillfully tooled in gold. The first he opened was a sixty-page treatise on the keeping of bees, London, 1610. He held the book in one shaking hand and studied the little woodcut of a beehive on the title page. The next book, a shelf down, was a 1588 work on the art of navigation, then 1552 on how to graft fruit trees, 1622 on the manuring of fields, 1650 on the care of horses, 1592 on the medicinal properties of herbs. All had Karlsson's bookplate on the inside front cover: intertwined initials in gold leaf on crimson leather.

"Wonderful, aren't they?" Stubblefield said over Sam's shoulder. "He sent most of them to England to be bound like that, unfortunately. I think he realized only later it would have been best to keep them in their original bindings. Like not removing the finish on an antique chair, you know."

Sam ran tobacco-stained fingertips over the grained leather surface of one of the little books. "I'm impressed."

"Look at this," Stubblefield said from the next bookcase. "And wait till you see the Dickens. I'm so envious."

Down the wall the glass doors stood open as though they had been commanded to attention. Sam took the heavy volume Stubblefield held out to him, cradled it expertly on his forearm and the globe of his stomach, and opened the leather cover: Newton, *Principia mathematica*.

"My, my," Sam said. He turned the crisp pages. "First edition. London, 1687. Very nice. Very nice indeed."

"This whole case is just full of the most ..."

"Alfred, why don't you go sit with the others," Sam said. "I don't want you pointing out things."

"Indeed. Very well then," Stubblefield said, raising his chin a bit. "I'll just ... well I'll just see about the correspondence. How would that be?"

"Fine, Alfred, fine." Sam slipped the Newton back into place and pulled out a volume at eye level: Gilbert's *De magnete*, London, 1603. He had seen the great book before, but next to it were three later editions, one of which he hadn't known existed. Completely absorbed, he took down book after book of classic works in science: Galileo, Bacon, Hooke, Harvey. He examined more carefully Newton's *Optics*, remembering the copy he had sold last year to Dennis Martin for $15,000. This copy was almost perfect, in the original calf binding, whereas the other had been rebacked rather crudely.

He moved on to other cases containing ten Shakespeare quartos, the Coverdale Bible, multi-volume voyage accounts, seventeenth-century almanacs in exquisite bindings, massive natural history books with hand-colored plates: Catesby, Jacquin, Besler, Alexander Wilson; first editions of the great nineteenth-century British writers: Austen, the Brontes, Dickens, Thackeray.

"Aren't the Dickens superb?" Stubblefield said over Sam's shoulder. He had apparently been watching for him to reach the case. "All in original parts, as crisp as the day they were published."

Sam pulled one off the shelf: *Our Mutual Friend.* The box the parts were in was made of grey buckram over boards with a crimson leather label on the spine. "This is like yours," Sam said. "The box, I mean."

"It is, it is," Stubblefield said. "Very similar. But they all are, aren't they: generic, these kind of boxes. Probably some bindery in Chicago."

"Did you find the correspondence, Alfred?" Sam asked, as he examined the Dickens.

"Yes, yes. There's a filing cabinet. You'll have to decide what you want."

When he came to another case of science books Sam recognized the Robert Boyle collection immediately. The first one he opened contained the ornate bookplate of Hugh Montclaire on the inside front cover, beside which old man Karlsson had pasted his own, smaller bookplate. Many of the others, but not all, had the Montclaire bookplate. The old man had obviously tried to collect all Boyle editions, and had

purchased a number of them in the Montclaire sale. Odd, Sam
thought, the same bookplate as the little book at Alice's.
Karlsson must have missed out on it to someone else at the
sale.

Behind him Sam could hear angry voices arguing,
Stubblefield and Vandersteen, but he was too absorbed in the
books to listen. As he turned title page after title page of books
whose rarity he was well aware of, he began to want them, not
to own, but to sell. In his entire career, he had sold only one or
two books to match them. Could he persuade Karlsson to sell
the books instead of giving them to the university? Persuade
Karlsson to let him sell the books on consignment? There's no
way I could buy them outright, but maybe, if I agreed to only a
modest commission, he might ... Except when he finds out
what the books are worth he ...

Sam jumped and almost dropped the book he was holding
when next to him Karlsson said loudly "Well, what do you
think? Are these things worth anything?" knowing full well
that they were.

Sam, chin down, looked up as though over the tops of
glasses at the big man next to him. "Oh yes indeed," he said. "I
should say so. It really is quite an amazing collection."

"Good, good." Karlsson dry-washed his hands. "So how do
we proceed with this? You say you need a list, or ...what did
you call it ... catalog? Where's that daughter of mine? She's the
one knows most about all this."

Otto Vandersteen, still in his London Fog, approached
casually, with his usual air of being about to whisper
something inappropriate. "Are we about finished here?" he
asked. "I would really like to be home in time for dinner."

"Where did Clarence go?" Stubblefield asked, looking
around the room.

"Here you are," Karlsson said as Karla and Audie came
through the door, laughing. "We were about ready to send out

a search party. Show Mr. Ives this catalog thing you were talking about."

"The island's so beautiful, Dad," Karla said. "Isn't it, Audie? The trilliums are all out on the trail up to the cliff. Hundreds and hundreds."

"I'm sure," Karlsson said. "He needs the letters and other stuff, too. We don't have all day here, Karla."

"Alright, Dad. You're so impatient. You should show Mr. Ives the island, at least." Her short hair had been disarrayed by the wind and the tight skin over her cheekbones was pink from early sunburn or from wind. She was holding one elbow. "We took a tumble," she said, nodding at Audie, who looked down at his skinned knees.

"For heaven's sakes, the files are over here," Vandersteen said. He marched toward the big desk. "Sam, come and see what you want, so we can get out of here."

"I'll just go look for Clarence," Stubblefield said. "He's acting most childish, if you ask me. He pouts, you know."

Half an hour later they were walking toward the door: Audie and Karla each with three drawers full of three-by-five cards cradled in their arms, Karlsson carrying a cardboard box of manila folders, and Sam a leather-bound photo album with pictures of the house, some of the books, old man Karlsson standing by his desk, when Elmer Stroud stopped them in the doorway.

"Maybe you folks better come see what this chubby fellow's all worked up about," he said casually. "Looks to me like he's about to start bawling, or throw up or something."

Alfred Stubblefield met them halfway up the concrete stairway: red-faced, hand on his chest, breathless. He swallowed twice, noticeably. "There's a body," he gasped. He forced another swallow. "Floating in the water. I think it's Biedermann. Gawd."

They left what they were carrying on the pier next to the boat. Audie and Karla ran ahead after Stubblefield told them "down the path along the shore, where the first outlook is." The others followed, not running but walking fast, with Stubblefield in the rear, still breathless, lifting his legs clumsily, as if he were in shallow water and trying not to get his pants cuffs wet. The stony path entered a maple woods, light green with spring leaves. Crowds of trillium like tiny nuns in white habits flowed around lichen-stained rocks and fallen tree trunks covered in moss. The path became steeper and swung closer to the lake shining in sunlight through the trees. Sam, behind Karlsson, could see ahead a block of sunlight where the trees opened suddenly. When they reached it, a rock ledge jutted out into a limitless view of the great lake. A low stone wall had been built along the edge. Karla was leaning over it, hands flat on the wall's rim, elbows locked. They gathered around her. Sam noticed Biedermann's maroon beret at the foot of the wall.

"Oh, he's down there," Karla said, looking up at them. "Audie's gone down."

Sam leaned over the wall, pressing the front of his thighs against the stone. Fifty feet down, at the foot of the cliff, waves rolled up onto a gravel beach and hissed to an end, almost surrounding a face-down body in beige sweater and brown corduroys rocking slightly in the receding water, white hair like old newspaper pulled seaward. Further down the shore, out of the trees, Audie appeared and began to run, stumbling and running again on the rough gravel of the beach.

"It's Mister Bierdermann, isn't it," Karla said as if to herself.

"I told you, I told you," Stubblefield said. He was standing behind the others. "He's drowned, isn't he. Oh Clarence, Clarence, you foolish man."

They watched as down below Audie rolled the body over. He stood and looked up at them, as if asking what to do, then shrugged his shoulders, got behind Biedermann's head, and, stooping to get him under the arms, dragged him up out of reach of the waves.

"Go call for a doctor," Karlsson said to no one. He looked around at them. "Karla, go back to the house and tell Stroud to get a doctor out here."

"It's too late for that," Vandersteen said. "He's certainly dead."

"It might be better to get the police," Sam said. He picked up Biedermann's beret and set it on the stone wall.

"The police," Stubblefield said. "Why on earth the police?"

"Sam's right," Karlsson said. "They'll have to know what happened. There should be a doctor or coroner or something too. Go on Karla."

"What should I tell him?"

"Tell him ... Oh, damn it, I'll go myself. Come on. Of all the damn things to happen."

Vandersteen sat on the stone wall, his back to the lake. "Good lord, we'll never get out of here now."

From down below, Audie called something they couldn't hear. Sam waved at him to come up.

"Did you see it, Alfred?" Sam asked. "See what happened?"

Stubblefield covered his eyes with one hand and shook his head. His jowls wobbled. "I was calling and calling: Clarence, Clarence. I knew you all wanted to leave. I don't know what made me go out on the point here. Such a striking view, I suppose. I don't know why I looked down like that. And there he was. How horrible. This wall is so low. He must have leaned over too far. He was always so clumsy: Clarence. Poor, poor clumsy Clarence. Then I ran to get you."

Audie came up the path, out of breath. His shorts were wet to the hips and his T-shirt water stained. Beach sand crusted his knees. "I didn't know what else to do," he said to Sam. "That guy's pretty much dead."

# SEVEN

"It's the silver one," Otto Vandersteen said as they walked through the van-pool lot. "The Audi." The night air smelled of coming rain. They walked in bluish light shed by poles arching over them. Cones of tiny insects rose to the lights. Vandersteen had parked the car at a slight angle at the end of a row because it was only two months old and needed to be safeguarded yet from dings. Stubblefield walked slightly behind him, almost touching him, as if he too needed safeguarding by the much smaller Vandersteen.

"Alfred! You're stepping on my heel," Vandersteen said. He moved away and lifted his foot to look over his shoulder at his heel.

"Sorry," Stubblefield said, preoccupied. His red windbreaker was still zipped up to his double chin; his khaki slacks were muddied at the cuffs and water-stained and not really wrinkle-proof after all.

Vandersteen pressed a key chain and the doors of the Audi unlocked with a double beep. Inside, the car smelled of soft leather and citrus. In the cup holder between the leather seats Vandersteen kept a small bottle of air spray to take away the new car smell. As he backed out of the parking space he could see in the rearview mirror Audie and Karla talking to an attendant at the lighted booth at the other end of the lot. Sam and Karlsson sat in the idling Cadillac waiting for them.

"I think they might be giving him difficulties about the van," he said, still watching but letting the car move slowly ahead over the sidewalk and to the street.

Clarence Biedermann had been the only university-qualified driver for the van. Both Vandersteen and Stubblefield had protested that they were too upset to drive, so Audie had driven back, with Karla in the front next to him and Vandersteen and Stubblefield sitting silently in corners in back. Sam and Karlsson had followed in the Cadillac.

"Nice car," Stubblefield said absently. He touched the walnut dashboard. "How much did it cost?"

Vandersteen turned the car into the street and didn't say anything until the stop sign at the corner. "Did you see him, Alfred?" he asked, looking straight ahead. "Jump?"

"I told you, I don't want to talk about it anymore," Stubblefield said. He laid a palm on his forehead to check for fever. "You heard what I told that policeman, or whatever he was. You can't imagine the shock, looking down and seeing him there, washing about in the water. I'll probably never be able to forget it."

"It had something to do with Roger, didn't it." Vandersteen said.

"Roger? What on earth are you talking about?"

"I'm talking about Clarence jumping. Whether you actually saw him or not, you know he didn't just stumble and fall over that wall, for gods' sake. All day he was acting worried about something."

"He was just angry at having to go to the island. He'd had more than enough of Mr. Karlsson. And what could Roger have had to do with it?" Stubblefield asked.

"Roger was baiting Clarence about something last night", Vandersteen said, "at your dinner. It had to do with Clarence going to Spain. His research grant."

"He just likes to tease people sometimes," Stubblefield said.

"I'd hardly cause it teasing. How well do you know Roger, Alfred?"

"What a stupid question. We live together. And if you want to get so nosy, don't think I don't know about your having dinner with him."

"Dinner? I don't know what you mean," Vandersteen said.

"Last fall. At Porta Bella."

"That." Vandersteen frowned, as though trying to remember. It had started to rain and he switched on the windshield wipers. "He came up to Rare Books one afternoon. Introduced himself as a friend of yours. I gave him a little tour and then he said he had some books to sell, I might be interested in. We were about to close, so we went for a drink at Porta Bella and stayed for dinner. I'd forgotten all about it. Why do you mention that now?"

They had turned into the traffic of University Avenue and were surrounded by cars and a city bus so close to Stubblefield's door he could have reached out and touched it. Spray from the wet blacktop rose in mist to the headlights.

"Books?" Stubblefield said. "Where would Roger get books to sell? Roger doesn't read. Probably my books. He seems to think what's mine is his. We had a big fight night before last because I sold some books I didn't have room for anymore. A shabby old encyclopedia, some paperbacks. To Alice, poor dear. He stormed out of the house when he found out. To tell the truth I rather dread going home right now. Roger's moods sometimes last forever."

"He didn't show it last night, at your dinner," Vandersteen said. "Although I did see you two arguing in the kitchen." He waited a moment before he said, "I thought at the time it might have something to do with his lady friend."

"What? What lady friend?"

Vandersteen smiled slightly. "You didn't know? I thought that might be the case."

"What lady friend?"

"Well, I don't know anything about it, of course. Perhaps it was just someone he works with. Although they did seem quite intent on each other."

Stubblefield began unaware to chew the fingernail on his thumb. "Where was this?"

"Oh it's nothing, Alfred. I only mention it because you seemed so concerned about Roger's mood."

"Where was it you saw them? Did you know her?"

"Quite an attractive woman, actually. Not anyone I had ever seen before, no. They were having coffee on the Union terrace yesterday afternoon, before your little dinner party. Actually, they seemed to be arguing about something. The woman was quite upset."

Stubblefield inspected his chewed nail and grunted. "I see. Well, Roger was behaving despicably before the dinner. I was worried he'd embarrass me. I assumed he was still angry about my selling the books." He looked out the side window as they passed the campus. "Perhaps it was something else."

Vandersteen signaled left to turn out of the traffic on University Avenue and into the side streets of College Heights. "Where did you meet Roger, Alfred?" he asked. He shifted into lower gear as they started up the steep hill to Stubblefield's house. The rain had become heavier; streetlights shone through webs of wet leaves.

"Why are you so interested in Roger all of a sudden? I'm not discussing my personal life with you, Otto, if that's what you're after."

"He's from California, isn't he? They can be quite...what? ruthless, out there. Hollywood, and all that. How well did Roger know Clarence?"

Vandersteen pulled the car to the curb in front of Stubblefield's house, and Stubblefield opened the door immediately. A light came on somewhere in the car.

"I've no idea what you're talking about," Stubblefield said. He heaved his bulk toward the door, then turned back. "By the way, Ives pointed out that the box on the Dickens you sold me looks very much like the boxes old man Karlsson had made for his Dickens."

"Oh? Well, it's a perfectly ordinary box.  No doubt from Mitchell's in Chicago. They produce similar ones for us on order still today."

"Roger thinks ..."

Stubblefield ducked his head to look past Vandersteen. A porch light had been turned on over the front door.

"Roger thinks what?" Vandersteen said.

"He's home, at least. God forbid he's still in a mood. I've had enough emotion for today."

"It's raining, Alfred. Wait till it slows. I want to talk to you yet."

Stubblefield pushed the door open wide and heaved himself out of the car into the rain. "Thanks for the ride." He slammed the door and hurried through the headlights, both hands on top of his head against the rain, bulky body swaying in his awkward attempt to run.

Vandersteen sat behind the wheel watching Stubblefield in the stairwell pull at the sticking door until it opened and he disappeared inside. Rain pounded on the car's roof and large drops exploded on the windshield and the silver surface of the hood. The car's headlights sliced cones of rain out of ghostly sheets.  Vandersteen started the engine.

"Roger thinks what?" he said to himself as he drove slowly up the street.

℘

Followed by a flight of finches, June Roth carried her TV dinner on a tray through the ghosts of furniture in the living room and into her father's library. Earlier, the sun had disappeared behind clouds, but the room was bright from all the lights she had turned on. Rain sounded on the leaded glass of the windows. She set the tray down on her father's desk and pulled his chair under her. The bust of Einstein, the antique wooden box where he had kept paperclips and rubber bands, the giant conch shell they had found on the beach that winter in Florida when she was twelve: all remained carefully arranged on the polished surface of the desk. Three of the finches fluttered to the desk and hopped toward the tray, their tiny nails clicking; others sat on her shoulders, one in the tangled nest of her hair. On the tray, Healthy Choice chicken Alfredo steamed in its container, an un-buttered half bagel held down a paper napkin, and a glass of red wine had slid precariously to a corner.

June Roth sipped the wine and reached to pull *Booked for Life* from between the bookends on the desk. She propped it up unopened against the conch shell, with her father's photograph on the back of the dust jacket facing her. A finch hopped onto the rim of the tray to peck at the bagel. June pushed it away and said, the wine glass still at her lips, "You know you don't like that, Timmy. You'll just make a mess."

Startled at the ringing of the phone, she spilled a little wine onto the tray. The birds scattered, peeping and chirping, through the doorway to the living room. She waited for the third ring, in case it was a telemarketer.

"This is June Roth," she said, and listened. She watched the spilled wine reach the paper napkin and begin to soak it pink. "I'll be here all evening. What is it about?" Listening, she started to pull apart the soaked edges of the napkin with a fingernail. "So it was you, then, sent the note. About Father's books." She stared at the oil painting of her father over the fireplace. "I won't tolerate it. I don't know what you ... Very well, then, in an hour. A cassette player? I do not. No, I do not." She listened. "He had a stereo system. I suppose there might be one there. I don't know. And what you've implied is completely false ... and vicious. There isn't a soul would believe such a thing. Such a vicious lie. My father was famous. My father was ..."

She held the phone away from her face and looked at the mouthpiece as if the hang-up click had come from someone standing just inside the black plastic. She put the phone back in its cradle and pulled open the desk drawer. The small envelop rested on a litter of papers, notebooks, printed reports; June Roth and the address of her condominium had been typed on an old machine with a faded ribbon. She took out the single sheet of paper. Torn from a cheap stationary pad, the top edge retained bits of gumming. Typewritten, unsigned, the note read: I will be in touch with you shortly concerning your father's theft of rare books. I am certain we can come to some agreement to keep this matter private.

She became aware of how her heart was beating, and touched her chest. She stared at the congealed gloss of the chicken Alfredo in its plastic microwave dish.

The gun. What did I do with the gun?

She stood and stayed a moment behind the desk staring at the note.

My purse. It's still in my purse from last night.

She started toward the living room.

I don't even know if it's loaded. You fool. I never even looked to see if it's loaded.

As she approached the doorway, the finches returned in a flock to flutter about her and she smiled up at them as if she were, she thought, a kind of saint, a savior.

ೞ

Whenever she entered the university library at night, Margaret Sawyer always had the disconcerting feeling this institution she directed had somehow after sunset been invaded by a hostile country whose swarming adolescent troops (male and female) were all more desperately intent on occupying each others' bodies than they were the building. She was the foreigner. No one recognized her, not even the night janitors. The girl at the entrance gate asked to see her I.D.

She plowed her way stoutly through the lounging groups of students: some at the computer terminals, some at elevators, others sitting on the floor or backed against walls; backpacks everywhere, like lugged-along babies they had been forced to guard. The whole area smelled of used air, of t-shirts and cutoffs and sneakers damp from the outside drizzle, of perfume and aftershave, of anxious young bodies unwashed since morning.

She avoided the bank of public elevators and went into the sorting room where returned books were shelved and used her key to the staff elevator. On the almost deserted third floor she unlocked the door to the administration offices. She closed it again but left it unlocked and, looking at her wristwatch, walked past the reception desk and down the night-lit corridor to her own office. She unlocked the door and fumbled on the wall for the light switch. The room flickered into light from florescent tubes hidden behind frosted glass in the ceiling. The room was tropical with an abundance of house plants on all flat surfaces: the marble window ledges, the front edge of her desk, the tops of filing cabinets, open spaces on the built-in book shelves; all crowded with Boston fern, rubber plants, fiddle leaf fig, philodendron, blooming orchids, a scarlet Amaryllis in gaudy flower. The room smelled of potting soil and wet moss and stones, like a creek bed.

Margaret Sawyer crossed to the wall of night-darkened windows and walked along the window ledge, habitually testing with one finger the dampness of the dirt in pots. She looked down on the mall between the library and the university bookstore where miniature people moved among the food carts and kiosks. She glanced at her watch again and sighed and ran her hands down her hips as if to smooth the dark blue slacks she wore, then brushed at a smudge left from the plant dirt on her fingertips. She felt a deep craving for the cigarettes she had given up eight years ago, when she had first arrived to be Director of Libraries and to start another life. Thomas had moved on to a new wife; Anne was in college in Boston and never heard from (bitterness, bitterness); the divorce settlement had left her enough to almost recover from the financial fiasco in which Thomas had gotten her involved. A new life. And now this.

She looked at her watch again: He said seven thirty.

Behind a mammoth desk of grey metal, she sat in the padded ergonomic chair. The casters squeaked a little on the plastic carpet protector. She pretended to look at papers. The black windows reflected the room inside. The sense of being in a foreign place persisted: no one talking outside her door, no phones ringing, no world outside the windows.

The wretched little man. Where is he? What could he possibly know? I thought it might be Otto, but, of course, Otto's too inept for anything of the sort. I should have kept the note.

The note had come a week ago. She had pushed it through the shredder, and now tried to remember the wording. We should have a talk about the Gateway contract. All those terminals for the library. Quite a sweet deal for someone, wasn't it. And then the phone call just before dinner.

She heard a noise in the hallway and her heart began to beat faster. She put her hand up to cover it. He knocked on the half-opened door and leaned in.

"Hello, Margaret," he said. "May I come in?"

She stood behind the desk. "Roger," she said, as though just having been introduced.

"What's this all about?"

෯

"Do you suppose I should call Pearl?" Alma asked.

When Sam hadn't returned from the trip north by eight, she had gone ahead and made her own martini and she sipped her second now, watching him eat the ham sandwich she had made him. He sat forward to the edge of his chair and bit into the sandwich as he leaned over the TV-tray, its crossed stork legs pulled up to his knees. He lifted his chin in non-answer and gripped the tall glass of beer on the corner of the tray as though he feared it might escape before he finished chewing and could drink.

"She has Klaus there, I suppose," Alma said. She pinched the pleat of her lavender slacks. Walt Whitman, on the rounded arm of her chair, reached his paw toward her martini. "He's always been such a strange boy, though: Klaus. I can't imagine he'd be much help at a time like this. She'd be the one to have to help him. Poor Pearl. Although I don't think Clarence and his son were ever very close. What do you think, Sam? Should I call? It's rather late now. No, I really think it best to see her in the morning. Wait til morning and go over there. I'm sure the last thing she wants now is to hear the phone ring. Stop that Walt."

She pushed the big cat down and it crossed to Sam and sat at the foot of the TV tray, looking up at him.

"What did the police tell her?" Alma asked. "I certainly hope they told her it was an accident. Whether it was or not."

"I don't think for a second it was an accident," Sam said, the beer glass paused in front of his mouth. He drank and reached for the sandwich. "Even Clarence couldn't have managed to fall over a cliff. There was a wall there, for one thing. Even if it was a low one. And he took his hat off, for another. No, he jumped. I wouldn't have thought he had it in him." He bit into the sandwich, then tore off a piece of the protruding ham and dropped it to the waiting cat.

"The man was upset about something. I didn't much notice it at the time, but thinking back ..."

"Sam." Alma stirred an olive around in her martini. "Maybe I know what was bothering him."

"Hmm?" Sam mumbled through a full mouth.

"This afternoon I was going down the hill to meet a student for coffee on the Union terrace, about three? And Roger Limbert caught up with me, all out of breath—you'd think he'd been running up the hill instead of walking down. You know how dramatic he can be. And asked if we could have coffee, he had something he wanted to talk about. Talk to me about as chair of the department. I told him I was meeting someone. I really don't like that man, Sam. He has this little smirk all the time, as if he knows something secret about you."

"You're the one always defending him," Sam said.

"Well then he said could we meet after work—he works in the Dean's office, you know: secretarial assistant or assistant secretary or whatever (he's always telling you), for a drink perhaps. Imagine that. I said I didn't think I could, I had meetings, couldn't he just walk along now and talk to me. What is it about, anyway? No, he didn't want to do that. He'd only say it had to do with Clarence Biedermann, some problem with his travel expense report from his trip to Spain. And I asked had he talked to Clarence about it and he said, no, it wasn't his place to do that. He'd call me tomorrow for a time we could get together. Then he turned and went back up the hill. Now don't you think that's odd? And I thought later that really he had no business discussing Clarence's expense report with anyone but his supervisor. I think that's very odd."

"Well, if he hadn't said anything to Clarence about it," Sam said, "then that couldn't have been what was bothering him. Even if it was, you don't jump off a cliff just because you've padded an expense account a bit."

"Roger seemed so very ... well, I suppose you would say nervous. He gave the impression of looking over his shoulder while he talked, if you know what I mean." Alma put her empty glass down on the rug and the cat went immediately to lick it. "The more I thought about it," she said. "Remember at the dinner table last night? Clarence was sitting next to Roger and Roger brought up something about Hemingway and Clarence's research grant."

Sam rubbed his mouth with his handkerchief. "That was an excellent sandwich. Thank you, dear. I was starved." He lit a cigarette and blew smoke over his head. "Now I'm going to have an after dinner drink. You want another?"

"No. Well, maybe. No, that was already my second."

From the drink cabinet Sam said, "Don't you have those kind of papers in the department office? His grant proposal, his travel report. I would think you would have to approve that sort of thing."

"Well, yes, I sign them. That doesn't mean I read everything. Especially travel reports. I'll look tomorrow."

"That Roger of yours is a busy fellow," Sam said. He dropped into his chair again and held his glass high to avoid the cat who had immediately sprung into his lap. "Get down, Walt. Nick told me this morning that he showed up at the pool where Nick was swimming; wanted Nick to meet him tonight for a drink."

"Really," Alma said, amused. "What did Nick do?"

"It seems Roger is a friend of Nick's old girl friend. This girl friend—Nick's been seeing her again, too—is Alice Lowell's sister." Sam glanced at his wristwatch. "I should call Nick. Find out what happened." But he took a drink of his Scotch and moved his hips deeper into his chair. "Except I'm too tired. It's been a long day."

"What was the book collection like?"

"Very impressive. Very, very impressive, in fact. Quite amazing, really, to see such books on an island in the north."

"Anything American?"

"Mark Twain. There was a lot of Mark Twain."

"That doesn't count. Any women?"

"Well I didn't look at everything, dear. The man was very eclectic."

"What was all that stuff Audie carried up?"

"The old guy's correspondence, records of books, where he got them and what he paid. I should go start work on them, I suppose. Except I'm too tired."

"Audie was in a hurry to go. I would have fed him."

"His girlfriend was in the car waiting. With her father. Audie drove Stubblefield and Otto back in the van and we picked him and his girlfriend up at the lot."

"Nick is seeing a girl again? Seeing her seriously?"

"He claims not. But who knows with Nick. He'll probably fall desperately in love again. I'm not sure I can take another of his affairs."

"Poor Nick. I do wish he'd find the right one."

Sam laughed. "He's got this dog now. Alice Lowell's dog, Belle. I think he's fallen in love with the dog."

"He's too soft-hearted for his own good. You'd think he'd learn."

Sam roughed the head of the big cat purring now in his lap. "But we like him, don't we, Walt. Nick's a good guy."

# EIGHT

Years ago Gino's had been just a neighborhood bar in the old Italian district, three buildings down from the Italian Workingmen's Club. There had been a Catholic church, St. Anthony's, a block away, on the other side of what had since become one of the main thoroughfares through town, just south of the university campus. Redevelopment crept in, with one or two small apartment buildings squeezed onto narrow lots where once houses had been so close to their neighbors that the old couples who lived there could sit on their sagging front porches and talk to the couple next door without even getting up and going to the porch rail. Children grew up and became lawyers or policemen or insurance salesmen. Old people died and developers bought their crumbling houses. St. Anthony's moved to a modern new building just off the beltway where there was sufficient parking.

Gino's on the corner by the stoplight had been sold to a recently retired couple who had tried to retain the building's outward charm, if not its interior or its usual costumers. Remodeled with much wood and chrome in art deco style, its patrons now were university and state government people, with occasionally a few anxious students on first dates or with visiting parents.

Nick hated the place but Karen had loved it, so Gino's was where she had met him after work almost every night those first few weeks. He hadn't been back since she left him. Before he had even opened the door, while he waited on the corner by the stoplight where backed-up cars were strung like beads on headlight beams, their metallic colors glossed by the rain that had begun to fall, he had felt an almost automatic defense building against any emotion that might hit him when he entered. But the defense didn't work. In the entryway, he turned down the wet collar of his jacket and felt his heart start to pound just as it had in the beginning when he would look around for her, not certain she would really show up this time.

The place was crowded. The marble bar had a chrome facing that had always reminded Nick of a car bumper. People sat on aluminum-legged stools with charcoal leather seats. Behind the bar a young woman in a maroon shirt stood waiting for a blender to finish working, while at the service end a young man in a similar maroon shirt handed a tray of beer in pilsner glasses to a waitress in a maroon shirt.

Nick studied the people at the bar as he walked behind them. Some turned to look at him. A woman smiled. He walked up the three steps to an upper, windowless room where booths lined two walls and a circular bar filled the center. He looked around, beginning to wonder if he remembered what Roger Limbert looked like.

"Here I am, Nick," she said, putting her hand on his shoulder from behind.

He turned so quickly he knocked her arm away. She had sounded so much like Karen that he, for the first time in his life, felt his knees weaken.

"Claire," he said. "You surprised me."

"I'm in the booth over there." She took his arm as if to lead him, then dropped it quickly and rubbed her bare arm. "Ooh, you're wet."

"It's raining out," he said.

She was wearing a sleeveless red dress that fit perfectly her slender body. The dress was cut low enough to reveal the beginning slope of her breasts. Every visible part of her skin was evenly tanned. Her blond hair was carved in hair spray.

"What are you doing here?" Nick asked.

"Come on, before someone takes the booth."

She was already walking away from him. Nick took a last look around the bar for Roger Limbert and followed her. She

THE DEGRADATION OF GOLD   159

sat in the corner of the booth with her forearms on the black onyx of the tabletop. Nick started to slide in opposite her.

"Take your jacket off, Nicki," she said. "Gads."

Still sitting, he pulled the jacket off and wadded it up beside him. She was smiling at him, her small hands folded together, smiling as if she were a young girl out for the first time with someone she really liked.

"So," Nick said. "I take it you're here in place of your buddy Roger."

She laughed. "Roger said he didn't think you'd come." She became coy. "I was beginning to think so, too. I've been here almost an hour. It's embarrassing to be sitting alone for almost an hour."

"I bet you had plenty of chances for company."

She began to fool with a cocktail glass she had pushed aside when she sat down. An olive floated among melting ice cubes. "Well, yes. But I think they were beginning to think I'd been stood up. It was embarrassing, Nick. You want a drink?" She looked around for a waiter.

"What's this about, Claire?"

"You never will say Clarisse, will you. It's so like you, Nicki. You just hate anything to be different. I remember that about you."

"How do you know Roger Limbert?"

"From California." She patted her hair as if she thought it might have moved. "He's a friend from California."

"What kind of friend?"

She pushed her hand at him in a habitual way he had once loved. "Oh, Nick, you don't have to worry about Roger."

"I'm glad I don't have to worry."

"Roger's from here. That's how we got to know each other, at a party one time. I said I was from here and he said oh, he used to live here, too. He was working for David Geffen then. You've heard of him, surely, the big producer? I mean, Roger wasn't any kind of big deal, just some kind of secretary, but he knew a lot of people. It's very important out there, Nicki, to know a lot of people." She studied the backs of her hands, inspecting her nails. "Roger knew about people, too. He'd poke me with an elbow and say, like, 'See that guy over there talking to the redhead?' and then he'd tell me something scandalous about him. I mean, he was kind of a gossip, really."

"So why'd he come back here?"

She shrugged. "Oh, I don't know. To live with this friend of his, I guess. Some professor he knows from a long time ago. To tell the truth, Nick–I mean, I like Roger, and all–but he's kind of a leech. I shouldn't really talk like that about him. He was always nice to me. Except once he tried to borrow money from me. From me. If you can imagine that." She laughed and pushed her hand at him.

A young man in a maroon shirt stopped at the booth and said, "So, what can I get you folks?" sounding as if he had finally managed to reach them.

"Vodka martini," Claire said.

Nick looked at his watch, then up at Claire.

"Come on, Nicki," she said.

"Manhattan. Up." When the waiter had gone, he said, "Why are you here instead of Roger? Was this some kind of set up, so I'd see you again?"

She dipped a fingertip into the watery remains of the martini and then licked it. "No, Nicki. It's just, I saw Roger this afternoon and he told me he'd met you at the pool and that you were going to have a drink with him here tonight. So I said 'Can I come, too?' and he said why don't I just go because he didn't really think you would come anyway."

Nick looked at her but she continued playing with the martini glass and didn't meet his eye. "You're such a liar, Claire," he said.

"Nicki!"

She did look at him then and he saw something hard in her face that he had never seen before, or maybe had never admitted seeing.

She pulled herself up from slouching in the booth. "Why are you being so mean?"

"Limbert told me he had something he wanted to tell me about Alice getting killed. Why would he not show up?"

"Because you told him you wouldn't come."

They both leaned back as the waiter set their drinks down in front of them on little napkins. "That it, folks?" he asked.

"Fine," Nick said. He picked the cherry out of the glass and set it on the napkin. "Roger tells you everything, huh. How did he know I would be at the pool this morning? He's never been there before, that I saw. What's going on here, Claire? What does he know about Alice's death?"

She cupped the martini glass in front of her face and looked into Nick's eyes. "Clarisse," she whispered, and tilted the drink to her red lips. She kept looking at him over the rim of the glass. "I think," she said, putting the glass down, "Nick, I think it was Roger who killed Alice."

"Come on, Claire. He didn't even know Alice."

"Yes he did, yes he did. He used to go in her bookstore all the time, he told me. And she was just at his house–I mean, his partner's house–to buy some old books. So he knew Alice, alright. And I'm scared of him Nick. I'm really scared of him."

"Just slow down, okay. Why would he kill Alice?"

"I don't know, Nick, but I know he did. I know him, Nick. I know him. That's why I'm so scared. You've gotta help me, Nick."

"Help you what? You're talking crazy. Why are you scared of him?"

"Because he knows that I know what he did. This afternoon–when I saw him?–I was going to the bookstore to do what you said, see if I could find the financial stuff I'd need for a lawyer to help me with, but they had it roped off–the police did–with that crime scene tape, and I couldn't go in. So I was just going to leave when Roger came up and said 'Well look who's here, let's go have coffee.' I hadn't seen him since I was back, so I said okay and we went across the street–to Starbucks?–and he was saying how sorry he was about my sister, and all. And then after he bullshitted for a while, like he does, he says, 'I suppose you'll be in big bucks now, your sister being dead, and all, what with the house and the store, and all.' And I said 'None of your business, Roger.' And he gets that creepy little grin of his and says, 'Maybe I'll go back to L. A. with you, we could get together again.' Like there's any way I would do that. Roger likes the high life. He thinks 'cause I might have some money coming ..."

"Claire, what has any of this to do with Alice getting killed?"

She took too deep a drink of her martini and looked like she'd just been poisoned, bowing her head against the burn. "Gads," she said, her voice hoarse. "Because ..." She touched a watery eyelash with a fingertip. "Because ..."

"You think he killed Alice just so you'd inherit some money and then he'd hook up with you again? That's just nuts."

"Well, you don't know Roger. What did he say about me? At the pool."

"He didn't say anything about you. Just that he wanted to talk to someone about Alice's murder and I should meet him here. At nine. Then you show up instead."

"You know why? You know why, Nick, that I came? Because he said he told you if anyone wanted to find out who killed Alice you should talk to me, hinting, like, I was the one killed my own sister, if you can imagine that. Did he say that, Nick?"

"No," Nick said. "He didn't." He studied her face: a pink flush over her forehead, her carefully outlined eyebrows crushed into a frown, her eyes narrowing. He had seen that look before, when she had been about to go into one of those tantrums whose reasons he had seldom understood but that he had finally learned just to walk out on.

"Good, then. He said he told you that." She sat back into the corner of the booth and crossed her bare arms under her breasts and looked down at her breasts as if to see how they were arranged. "He's a goddamn liar, most of the time."

Nick kept watching her until she looked away from him. "Why would he say something like that, Claire?"

"Who knows. Probably he thinks he can scare me enough to get some money out of me. What a laugh. Why do you think I came back to this dumb place? Because I ran out of money, is why. Because I couldn't even pay the rent the last three months."

"You were going to live with Alice?"

"No. I just needed a place to stay. Till I figured out what to do. Jeez, Nick, what am I going to do? What a mess, my life. Maybe now, with the inheritance, I'll go to New York instead of back to L.A. Lots of people in L.A. said that was where I should've started: New York. I might be better on the stage than in movies. What with close-ups and all. What do you think, Nicki?"

Nick finished his drink. "I think it's time for me to go." He leaned forward to reach for his wallet. Claire sat up suddenly and touched his cheek with cold fingertips. He felt the slight scrape of her nails against his beard stubble.

"Nicki, don't go," she said.

How well he remembered that tone: teasing, fake pleading.

"You should come with," she said. "To New York. I just bet you've never even been to New York City. You could get a job there like nothing: they've got tons of police. It would be so exciting, Nicki. And we could get to know each other again, like old times."

"Sure thing," he said, getting up. "I'll think about it and let you know." He dropped a ten dollar bill on the table and reached for his jacket. He half expected her to call his name or even come after him as he went down the stairs into the even more crowded lower bar. But she didn't, and he pushed his way through standing groups all clutching beer bottles or drink glasses chest high and out the door into the spring night.

Another world: rain-washed air, headlights and streetlights gleaming on wet pavement, music from somewhere (open apartment windows or cars at the stoplight). The rain had stopped. Nick left his jacket open and the cool air blowing against him as he started up Regent Street made him realize he had been sweating, his shirt wet under the arms.

Go with her. Good god. And he began to wonder again at how he could have spent so many months of his life obsessed with someone for whom he now felt only contempt, how that slender body that once had squirmed so unavoidably in his thoughts whenever he was not with her could now mean nothing to him. And he thought of Karen and wondered what would have happened if she had stayed, wondered how he would feel were he ever to see her again.

He had left the commercial section of Regent Street and was walking past old houses with wide porches and old trees in front yards. The air smelled of wet grass and wet dirt in beds of pale tulips cupped closed against the dark. Earthworms sprawled on the wet sidewalk. Some had drowned in puddles where the concrete had sunk.

Could she have had anything to do with her sister's murder? That's just crazy. She wouldn't have been strong enough, for one thing; too squeamish, for another. Why didn't Roger show? Why did she show up instead of Roger?

He walked the dog when he got home. It had started to rain again so when he got back to the apartment he had to towel the dog off in the entryway with his handkerchief and wipe her paws and use the same handkerchief to dry his own hair before going up the two flights of uncarpeted stairs. The dog flopped down immediately on the old blanket he had given her for a temporary bed.

Claire said something about Roger selling some books to Alice.

He wanted to call Sam, but it was late. On the sofa he watched the last local news: a march down State Street by teaching assistants threatening a strike; the opening of a new office building in the Sauk industrial park; a truck turnover on the beltway; a university professor dead, possibly suicide. Wonder if Alma knew him. Then, after the weather, a late report: police had found a body by the lagoon in Vilas Park. Shot in the head. Possibly a drug deal. No further details.

ଔ

The sirens and the circling lights on top of the squad cars had waked the lions and the tigers and made the monkeys frantic on their island. The lions roared and paced in dark cages; the monkeys screeched and scolded and threw things into the moat; from inside a building somewhere jungle birds shrieked. The smell of rain soaked hides and wet manure hung in the air. Two squad cars, headlights still on, were parked one behind the other on the broad asphalt walkway leading from the zoo area down a slope to a man-made lagoon. In the triangulated beams of headlights, five men stood looking down at the body of a man lying on his back in the wet grass just at the edge of the walkway. A woman in a yellow rain slicker moved around the body taking pictures. Flashbulbs exploded light over the suddenly silver grass in the dark beyond the body. A siren in the distance became louder as it neared.

Detective Alvin Nielsen tipped an opened wallet toward the headlights and pressed the plastic film over the driver's license. He couldn't read it. He pressed his eyes with fingertips. He felt the liquor inside him yet. The phone had jarred him out of sleep in a recliner. He blinked and tried again to read the license. "Roger Limbert," he said, turning to look back at the body, as if now he recognized it.

A young cop holding an unnecessary flashlight had squatted by the body. The suede jacket, stained dark by the rain, was unzipped over a pale peach silk shirt. The man's head was turned sideways on the grass and the grass under it was black with blood. One arm was twisted beneath him and the other, flung out on the grass, seemed to point at someone fleeing.

"I think it's a bullet hole," the young cop said. He pointed to a blackened spot the size of a prune half hidden by the man's thick hair.

An ambulance, blinking red lights but with the siren off now, turned slowly away from the zoo and rolled down the asphalt path toward them. Another car followed. Both vehicles stopped behind the squad cars and doors opened simultaneously. Two men in white went to the back of the ambulance. A stout man slammed the door of the car and edged sideways around the ambulance so as not to have to walk in the wet grass.

"I was sleeping," he said to Nielsen and pulled a hand down a round face. His raincoat was buttoned to the neck and Nielsen guessed he still had his pajama top on.

"Look him over, Marvin," Nielsen said, "before it starts raining again."

One of the ambulance attendants said, "How long's it gonna be?" He stood next to his partner and they held a stretcher on end between them. "We could wait inside."

Nielsen, ignoring them, said, "Where's that watchman fellow?"

"Right here." A man the size of a jockey stepped out from behind two cops in uniform. "Kin I go now? Them animals are going nuts." His voice was high, almost squeaky.

"Just tell me what you saw," Nielsen said.

"I already told that guy there."

"Well, tell it over to me. Okay?"

"I'll tell you right now I can't identify no one. Mainly I just saw the car."

"You saw a car. Where?"

"Right here. Where the guy's lying there. I come out to do my rounds ..."

"What time?"

"Ten-thirty. I start at ten-thirty on the dime. Anybody knows me knows ..."

"You saw a car down here at ten-thirty."

"Right. I wouldn't a looked but I heard this bang. Kinda muffled, but it sounded like a big firecracker. One of them cherry bombs, except muffled, like I said. So I went and looked down there and I seen somebody go past the tail lights, you know, just a shadow block out them red tail lights one after the other. And don't say what'd he look like, 'cause it was dark. I just saw this shadow. And I'm about to go down there 'cause nobody's suppose to be there. That ain't a road, you know. That's a walkway, even though the ground crew uses it for their vehicles. For the public, you know, it's just a walkway. Anyways, I'm about to go down there and he gets in the car and drives away and I just see the tail lights go out the park to Vilas Drive. So I thinks to myself, that's funny, but I go on and do my rounds, checking the animals, and I get done with the bird house there, and I think, well, maybe I'd better go down see what that fellow was up to. So I go down and here's this body lying there. Scared the bejesus out of me, for sure."

"You didn't see the car go by the zoo? By your office, or whatever?"

"No, I didn't. And that don't mean I was sleeping on the job, either. Anybody knows me knows ..."

"The car had to go right past your office to get down there."

"Well, more'n likely it did. Probably had the lights off, knowing he wasn't suppose to be there in a car. I watch the weather report, you know, ten-fifteen, and the sports, before my ten-thirty, so I might have missed him, he didn't have his lights on."

"You keep saying 'he'. You're sure it was a man?"

"Not sure at all. Like I say, it was dark. I just seen this shape. This shadow. Is all I seen. Could a been a woman, I suppose. Didn't really think about it."

"So you didn't see the two of them together, by the car, arguing or something."

"No. I just seen what I told you."

"What kind of car was it?"

"Now how'm I supposed to know that? From the tail lights?"

The coroner stood from squatting beside the body and came back to Nielsen and the watchman.

"What's the story?" Nielsen asked.

"Shot in the head." Wheezing, he took a deep breath and flexed one knee. "Damn arthur itis." He patted his stomach. "Getting too big a stomach to be squatting, besides. Anyway, looks like maybe he was dumped here. You'll have to have your guys look around. See if they can find the gun, any blood besides what's on him. Anyway, you can take him away, you want. I'm going back to bed."

"Kin I go now?" the watchman said. "I gotta get back up there."

"Go ahead," Nielsen said. "Marvin," he called after the coroner walking sideways past the ambulance again, "I'll talk to you in the morning."

Marvin raised his arm without turning back.

Nielsen walked over to the body of Roger Limbert and looked down at the waxy face, the bloodless lips.

"What were you up to, Roger Limbert," he said, "to get yourself killed like that?"

# NINE

Sam Ives couldn't concentrate on his *New York Times*. He realized he was merely looking at the article on a suicide bombing in Tel Aviv and had no idea what he had supposedly just read. He folded the paper and looked over his shoulder at the counter in the Brew Kup. He needed more coffee. Nick was already ten minutes late.

"This is a refill," he said to the girl behind the counter. He left a dollar, filled his red mug with coffee from one of the urns, and carried it back to the table in the window alcove. He wished now he had sat outside because he needed a cigarette, but the plastic chairs there were still wet from last night's rain. He was tired and irritable from not having slept at all. He had called Nick at six-thirty to catch him before he left the house.

"Nick, I need to talk to you. Will you be on the terrace at nine?"

"Not the terrace. I'm bringing the dog in with me. I can't bring her on the terrace."

"You mean to tell me we're never having coffee on the terrace again?"

"Well, not with the dog."

"Meet me at the Brew Kup then. At nine. I need to talk to you. You heard about Biedermann?"

"Who?"

"Clarence Biedermann. I'll tell you. I'll see you at the Brew Kup."

I suppose he can't bring the damn dog in here, either, Sam thought. He looked around. There were only two others in the room: students studying. He gathered up the sections of the Times and crammed them into his briefcase, grabbed a hand full of napkins from the metal dispenser, and carried his coffee outside. He had finished wiping dry two of the plastic chairs and the table top, grumbling, and was lighting a cigarette when he saw Nick and the dog a half block down. Damn dog, he muttered.

Nick handed him the dog's leash. "Here, watch her while I get some coffee. You look like you haven't slept in a week."

"I haven't," Sam said. Nick was already going through the door. The dog looked at Sam and held up its paw to shake. "You look worse than me, dog," Sam said.

"I don't have much time," Nick said. He set his coffee down and tested the seat of the chair for wetness. "What did you want?" His hair was still damp from swimming.

"I suppose you take that dog swimming with you, too," Sam said.

"Belle?" Nick looked down at the dog lying at his feet, head on its paws. "I wish I could. Labs love to swim. I tie her to a tree. She's really good about it."

"I'm glad."

"You're in a great mood this morning. What about this Biedermann?"

"He killed himself yesterday. Jumped off a cliff practically in front of me. Well, I didn't see it, but we found his body, washing around in the waves. Terrible sight." Sam hiked a shoe onto his knee and ground his cigarette butt out on the sole.

"You lost me," Nick said. "Where'd all this happen? Who's Biedermann?"

"I told you. We went up to the Peninsula yesterday to look at that book collection. Several of us, Biedermann included. He went off by himself while we were in the house and the next thing Alfred Stubblefield comes running in to say he saw Biedermann fall off a cliff. Well, he didn't fall, that's certain. The man jumped. The other thing, Nick: Alma says she ran into Roger Limbert on the hill yesterday and he was hinting maybe there was a problem with the way Clarence was reporting his travel expenses. Clarence was worried about something alright, all day. Now what business was that of Roger Limbert, to be telling that to Alma, who's Clarence's boss. Well, head of the department, anyway. But the thing that kept me awake last night, Nick, I kept thinking about the books. The Montclaire bookplate. You remember that Boyle book I showed you the other night, that came in the box with the encyclopedias? I was awake all night, thinking."

"Sam, calm down. You're losing me. Just tell me about Biedermann."

"I told you already. He killed himself. And Alma and I think it's because he'd been cheating on his expense account and Roger Limbert found out about it and was threatening to turn him in. I wouldn't be surprised if the little snake was blackmailing him. What happened with you last night? Did you meet him for a drink, like he wanted?"

"No. I didn't. I went there–Gino's–but he didn't show up. Claire did."

"Claire?"

"Alice Lowell's sister. I told you about her."

"Ah, Claire. The old girlfriend. She just happened to be there?"

"Limbert apparently told her he was going to meet me there. She showed up and he didn't."

"How does she know Roger?"

"Long story."

The dog sat up and put its paw on Nick's knee. Nick scratched its head. "Lie down now, Belle. You have to learn to be patient."

"What'd she want?" Sam asked.

Nick studied his coffee mug. "Sam, I think those two might have had something to do with Alice Lowell getting killed. I told you the reason Limbert wanted to meet me was about Alice. He said it was important, which is the only reason I went there last night–to Gino's. Then he doesn't even show and Claire's there instead, hinting that maybe Limbert was going to tell me that she's the one who killed Alice."

"Her own sister?"

"Then Claire turns around and says Roger's the one and she's afraid of him, I should help her."

"But why? Why would either one of them?"

"Money. Claire thinks she's going to inherit the house and the store and whatever else Alice had. Which is probably true. There's nobody else."

Sam grunted. "Hardly a fortune."

"It could look like it to somebody broke. Anyway, I've got to talk to Al Nielsen about it. He's probably talked to Claire already, but I doubt he even knows about Roger Limbert."

"Roger is beginning to look like even more of a snake than I thought."

Sam jerked his chair in as two students tried to squeeze behind him to one of the other tables. He bumped the edge of the table with his stomach and the coffee mugs skidded but didn't tip. The sidewalk was becoming crowded as more students headed toward the campus and the next class.

"The other thing I wanted to tell you, Nick ..." Sam began.

Nick was looking past him into the crowd moving toward them on the sidewalk. "Here comes Alma," he said.

Her lavender dress glowed among the disarray of washed out T-shirts and jeans. She was frowning, trying to find a way through the unhurried bands of students. She did not see Nick and Sam and would have passed them, but Nick stood up and said, "Alma."

"Oh my," she said. "Here you are." She leaned against the curve of the back of Sam's chair as students pressed by her.

Nick pulled his chair out and the dog up on its leash. "Sit down, Alma." He dragged the dog around to the chair opposite Sam.

"What a nice dog, Nick. What's its name?"

"Belle."

"Hello, Belle."

"What's wrong, dear?" Sam asked, frowning at her.

A city bus roared by, leaving a swirl of street debris and blue exhaust. Alma sat and waited for the noise to pass.

"I'm so glad I saw you," she said. "I thought you'd be on the terrace. Something awful has happened, Sam. I still can hardly believe it's true. Alfred Stubblefield called me just after you left this morning." She locked her hands together on the table top. "From the police station, Nick. Crying. Actually weeping. You know how he is. He wants me to find him a lawyer. He doesn't know any lawyers and says I'm to find him one immediately. Roger ... Roger's his companion, Nick; you don't know him ... Roger's been shot to death and they've arrested Alfred for it. Can you imagine such a thing?"

"My lord," Sam said. He pulled himself up from the slouch into which his heavy body had slid relentlessly on the chair's plastic.

"I don't know any lawyers," Alma said. "Alfred thinks because I'm department chair ... I suppose the university has lawyers, but not for something like this. Nick, you must know a lawyer. Poor Alfred sounded so desperate. As you can imagine. Anyone would."

"Limbert was shot?" Nick said, frowning. "Last night?"

"I don't know any details. Alfred said they came to the house ... the police ... in the middle of the night and asked him hundreds of questions about Roger without saying why and then one of the police came in and said there was blood all over the front seat of Alfred's car and they arrested him and he's been in jail since. Can you just imagine Alfred Stubblefield in jail? He must be devastated. Not just being in jail, but Roger ... oh my, Roger was his whole life. For the most part, anyway."

Nick looked at his wristwatch. "I'd better go try to see Al Nielsen." He stood and looked down at Belle. "What am I going to do with you? Well, you'll have to come with."

Sam pushed out of his chair. "I'm coming, too."

Alma looked up at them, alarmed. "But why? What about a lawyer? What am I to do about a lawyer for him?"

"Limbert was suppose to meet me last night, Alma," Nick said. "And he never showed. The police will want to know about it."

"But you don't even know him."

"I know him."

"Alma, dear," Sam said, "just go to the Dean's office and tell them the situation. They'll know what to do."

"I have a class right after lunch, too," Alma said, rising. "Poor Alfred. How really awful for him." Sam embraced her and she brushed habitually at something on his shoulder as they separated. "All this and Clarence Biedermann. The department will be in chaos this morning. I should probably cancel my classes. Pearl Biedermann called, too. I must say she seems more upset about Klaus than poor Clarence. He's gone into some sort of 'meditative trance' she called it: Klaus has. The boy was always peculiar. I asked her if she had any idea why Clarence would do such a thing and she said he's not been himself lately, worried–well, she said 'distracted'– distracted about something, he wouldn't say what. Nick, did Sam tell you about Roger yesterday? What he implied about Clarence?"

"Yes, he did," Nick said. The dog, sitting beside Nick's shoe, had put her paw impatiently on his knee. "Alright, Belle, we're going. Sam, maybe it'd be better if you stayed here."

"No, no, I have to go," Sam said. "This Nielsen of yours has been wanting to see me about that box of books. He'll probably try to arrest me again and I'll want you to be there."

"Don't be silly, Sam," Alma said.

"Well he did once, you know: arrest me." He lit a new cigarette and was about to throw away the match but pinched it instead and put it in his pocket.

"I don't know when I'll be home, dear," Alma said as she moved away into the crowded sidewalk.

Sam, Nick, and the dog stood on the curb as another bus passed, then crossed the street and started toward the state capitol building, its white, sunlit dome rising above the new leaves of the old trees on the capitol square. Street people lounged on benches at the bus stops, as anonymous as the sparrows that, dodging foot traffic, dashed from one discarded trifle to another. At the stoplight a man in a black suit offered tiny bibles while the woman next to him recited the gospel to the air.

Sam and Nick walked close to each other, their arms brushing occasionally as they moved to avoid oncomers. Belle trailed on leash behind, her head down as if very tired, or bored.

"So," Sam said, "now you know why Limbert didn't meet you last night."

"Maybe," Nick said. "Except he could have been killed after he was supposed to meet me."

"But what if he was killed to keep him from talking to you? You said he had something he wanted to tell you about Alice."

"That's what he claimed. We don't know anything yet, Sam."

"Alma said he was killed in Stubblefield's car. We know that much."

"No we don't. Alma just said the police said there was blood in the car. That doesn't mean he was killed there."

"Well, I can't really see Alfred killing anyone. It's pretty preposterous. He'd faint first."

"Sam, last night Claire mentioned something while we were talking. That Limbert knew Alice because Alice had been to their house to buy some books. I don't know whether she was buying them from Limbert or from his housemate. Didn't you say that Alice bought those books of yours–that encyclopedia–from someone the night before she was killed?"

"She did, yes," Sam said. "If she got them there they would certainly have been Alfred's. Roger would never have hauled an eleventh *Britannica* from California. Or ever own one, for that matter. But Alfred wouldn't mutilate books like that; cut the heart out of them. He's too much of a bibliophile."

Sam stopped suddenly. People following dodged past him, scowling.

Nick looked back. "What?"

"That little book by Robert Boyle that was in the encyclopedia."

"What about it?" Nick said. "Let's get around the corner. Out of traffic. Belle's getting stepped on."

They turned at the corner. At the end of the block loomed the City-County Building, clad in giant blue tiles.

Sam said, "Last night, I couldn't sleep, thinking about the trip to the Peninsula, the book collection there, Biedermann jumping–all that just kept going around in my head. The odd thing is, Nick, when I was looking at the books there, old man Karlsson's books, there was a whole shelf of books by Robert Boyle, and some of them had the bookplate of a Hugh Montclaire: very ornate coat-of-arms type, probably eighteenth century, I'd say."

"Who's Hugh Montclaire?"

"Doesn't matter. The thing is, the little book by Boyle I found in the encyclopedia had the same bookplate. Pretty odd, isn't it, that I'd see the same bookplate in two days, in different places. And all on books by Robert Boyle. So how did the one book end up in Alice's bookshop?"

"Sam, I don't have the faintest idea what you're talking about."

"This is a very valuable book, Nick. It's a great rarity. What I'm thinking is maybe it came from the Karlsson library. If it did, it was stolen."

"You think it was stolen? By who?"

"Ted Roth would have wanted it badly for his collection. It's a great rarity. But he's dead."

"Maybe he had it already and somebody stole it from him."

"Except he wrote his name in all the books in his collection, and I remember noticing specifically there was no signature in the little book at Alice's. No, I think it came from the Karlsson collection."

"Maybe your friend Stubblefield stole it. It was in his encyclopedia."

"Well, I doubt it. But he had been up there, several times, to look over the collection for the library. Along with Otto Vandersteen. And Biedermann, too, I believe."

They had stopped in front of the entrance to the City-County Building. Above them colored banners snapped in the breeze.

"Well, Belle," Nick said, squatting down to the dog's level, "I'm afraid you're going to have to stay here." He bumped foreheads with the dog, and tied its leash around the trunk of one of the young ash trees. "If anyone tries to untie you, bite him. No barking now." The dog looked up at him and then laid down.

Sam was holding the plate glass door open when Nick caught up with him. "Anyway," Sam said, "my theory is someone's been pilfering Karlsson's library. Except I wouldn't have really thought Alfred had it in him. Unless Alfred might have brought Roger Limbert out to the island with him. They were together, you know. 'Significant others.' Now Roger I could see as a thief."

"A dead thief," Nick said. "Let's just take the stairs. It's only down a floor."

Sam held onto the metal railing and watched his feet on the concrete steps. Nick pushed open the door and they entered a wide hallway. The wall to their left as they walked down the hall to the entrance to the police department was half glass. Behind it, men and women, some in uniform, worked at metal desks or stood talking to each other.

"This place makes me very nervous," Sam said.

"Is this where they brought you?" Nick said.

"It was through a back entrance somewhere. Is there another floor below this?"

"Off Wilson Street. That's where the holding cells are."

"I'm aware of that."

"They didn't put you in a cell, did they?"

"No, but it was very humiliating, Nick."

Nick opened the door to the department offices and Sam followed him to a long counter at which a young man seemed to be waiting for someone.

"Can I help you?" the young man asked.

"We need to see Detective Nielsen," Nick said.

The young man looked at a clock on the wall and said, "I think ..." He pressed something below him and brought a phone to his face. "Detective Nielsen. Two men here for you." He tucked the phone into his shoulder. "Who are you?"

"Tell him Nick Ash."

The young man repeated it, listened, then said, "Down that hall. Second door."

A cop in uniform came out of Nielsen's door as they approached. Nick recognized him as the young cop who had been in Alice Lowell's with Nielsen. He nodded to him as they passed in the hallway.

Nielsen stood up behind his desk as Nick and Sam entered. "Morning, Nick," he said. "Ah, and Mr. Ives. You I've been looking for." He didn't offer to shake hands and sat down again. "I want that box of books you took from the crime scene, according to Nick here. You seem to be trying to get yourself in trouble, Mr. Ives. You said nothing about those books when I had you in here the other night, did you."

"They were my books," Sam said. He patted the cigarettes in his shirt pocket. "I had no idea ..."

"Al, what we came about is the guy you found in Vilas Park last night," Nick said.

"Oh? You know something about that?"

"I knew the guy. We knew the guy." He looked up at Sam standing next to him. "Roger Limbert. I was supposed to meet him at nine last night at Gino's and he never showed."

Nielsen studied the two men. "Sit down," he said, waving at chairs in front of his desk. He picked up a paper clip and began to unwind it. The top of his metal desk was bare except for a stack of folders and, on the corner, a bust of Lincoln in black plaster. "So, tell me," he said.

"I didn't really know him," Nick said. "Sam's the one knows him. Like I say, he made contact with me yesterday and said he had something to tell me about Alice Lowell's death, I should meet him at Gino's. Then he never showed."

"That so," Nielsen said. "Interesting. And you've got no idea what it was he wanted to tell you?"

"None. But I thought you should know his getting killed might have something to do with Alice Lowell. We heard you made an arrest already."

"Now how'd you hear that? We just got the guy in here a few hours ago."

"My wife," Sam said. "My wife's a colleague of Stubblefield. He called her to get a lawyer for him."

"That right? You know him pretty well then? Stubblefield? How 'bout his friend, the dead guy? You know him, too?"

"Not well," Sam said. "They're my wife's friends, actually. But I really don't think Alfred Stubblefield would be able ... Well, he's hardly the violent type."

"What have you got on him, Al?" Nick said.

Nielsen flipped the deformed paperclip toward a metal wastebasket and it tinked on the side. He opened his desk drawer and shut it again. He leaned elbows on his desk and interlocked his big hands. "What have I got? I've got his car with blood all over the front seat, is what. Parked in his garage, too yet."

"What's he got to say? Did he say he did it?"

"Now, Nick, it's never that easy, is it. He says the two of 'em had a fight–just a word type fight, of course, nothing too violent, but loud, loud enough so the next door neighbor heard them–and then this Limbert fellow drove off in the car. Next thing Professor Stubblefield knows the police are knocking on his door. And his car is back in the garage, mysteriously, with blood all over the front seat. Now, like I said, he admits they had a fight. Seems Limbert was going to leave him. For a woman."

"Did he say what woman?" Nick asked.

"No. The guy's all shook. Won't talk anymore without a lawyer."

Nick glanced at Sam. "Something else you ought to know, Al. We were talking on the way over here that there might be another connection between Limbert and the Lowell murder. Sam's box of books. Or boxes of books. It's possible that Alice bought the books the night before she was killed, bought them either from Limbert or from Stubblefield. Sam says Stubblefield."

"That so." Nielsen swivelled his chair so he faced the wall, as if he wanted to show Nick and Sam the bald spot on the back of his head. The collar of his not-quite-white shirt was turned under in back. Sam looked at Nick. Nick shrugged.

After a minute without saying anything, Nielsen swung back to face them again and said to Sam, "The box of books you took, Nick says some of the books were hollowed out."

"Three of them were, yes," Sam said.

"You find anything in them?"

Sam inspected the backs of his hands. "Well, not in them, exactly. There was another, smaller volume that I suspect had been hidden inside of the larger volume, but had fallen out."

"What was that, this smaller volume?"

"An early tract by Robert Boyle, the English scientist. *Of the Degradation of Gold.*

"The what of gold?"

"Degradation. It has to do with the transmutation of mercury into gold. Alchemy. That sort of thing. A very rare book indeed."

"That so. Well that explains one thing. How about a plate full of finches?"

"What?"

Nielsen stood suddenly, sending his chair spinning. "You fellows stick here a minute," he said as he came around the desk and headed for the door.

"Are you going to tell him about Roger and your old girlfriend?" Sam asked Nick after Nielsen had gone.

"We'll see," Nick said.

Nielsen carried a metal box when he returned. The young cop they had passed in the hallway followed him, holding a portable radio out in front of his stomach as if it were a tray. Nielsen opened the box on his desk while the cop plugged in the radio. The cord didn't reach the desk and the cop stood holding the plastic radio, looking like a dog at the end of its leash.

"There's a plug there," Nielsen said. He motioned by half turning to the wall behind him. He had taken a tape cassette out of the box and was tapping it on the heel of his hand. "We found this in the glove compartment of the Professor's car," he said. "I want you to listen to it." When the radio was plugged in and on his desk, he inserted the cassette into the tape deck. For a few minutes there was no sound but the faint hiss of the tape moving.

Then: *"I'm not certain he's come in yet. Just one minute, I'll transfer you."*

A clicking of phones. *"Yes?"*

*"Well, I catch you in. I was afraid you might have left already."*

*"Left?"*

*"On your little trip to the island. You should have told me, Otto."*

*"What I told you was we have to do this slowly. I'm not about to walk out of there with a box of books under my arm."*

*"I totally agree. However, we can't afford to waste a trip. There won't be that many. Who are you going with?"*

*"Biedermann."*

*"Well, there's no problem then. Clarence has his own worries these day."* A laugh. *"Roth wants the little alchemy volume. You know what he means?"*

*"Probably* The Degradation of Gold. *He's babbled on about it more than once to me. He tried to buy it years ago but Karlsson got it first. He'll pay eight thousand."*

*"So, there's no problem then?"*

*"Unless I can't find it. There're thousands of books there, you know, and I don't know what this one looks like."*

*"Find it. He also wants something called the* Audubon finches *to give his daughter. You know what that is?"*

*"I'm not doing that. I know what he means. He wants one of the big colored prints of finches. She's nuts about finches, his daughter. Has live ones in her house, even. But the* Audubon *folios are huge. It would be hard to do it by myself. Besides, someone is bound to notice sooner or later that a plate is missing."*

*"Otto. We discussed this. Find what he wants. You can always say the set was incomplete when it came to the library. Anyway, nobody's going to miss a plate of finches, for gods' sake."*

*"The books will have to be appraised. If it's Sam Ives, he'll probably turn every page of every volume, knowing him. I told you in the first place it would be much safer to do this after the books are here and before they're processed."*

*"And what if Karlsson decides not to give the books after all?"*

*"Well, that's the chance we take."*

*"No. We don't. I won't be around forever."*

The tape hissed again and Nielsen leaned to the radio to turn it off.

"I can't believe it," Sam said. He was staring at the cassette player on Nielsen's desk as if the conversation had actually taken place there.

"I take it you know what that was all about," Nielsen said.

"That was Otto Vandersteen and Roger Limbert. I simply can't believe it. I was just telling Nick ... But I thought it might be Alfred. Even that seemed incredible enough. But Otto."

Nielsen opened his desk drawer and pulled out a clip board. He wrote something down and said, "Who's this Otto Vandersteen?"

"Curator of Special Collections," Sam said, still thinking. "At the university."

"Oh yeah. Kind of a foreign guy. I met him once before. And the other guy is our dead man. And you know both of them, Mr. Ives. Why don't you tell me what this is all about?"

"Yes. Alright." Sam looked at Nick. "I think I do know. They're talking about a collection of rare books that's being given to the university. A very valuable collection, put together in the thirties and forties by Jens Karlsson. His grandson is giving it to the university library. The island they mentioned is off the tip of the Peninsula. Karlsson has an estate there."

"Where a guy from here killed himself yesterday?" Nielsen asked.

"Yes. I was there myself, actually. Yesterday. Clarence Biedermann. They mentioned him in the tape."

"You know *him* too?"

"Yes, of course I do. He's a colleague of my wife in the English department. It was a terrible thing. I didn't actually see him ... well ... It was terrible."

"Go on about the tape."

"Well, it's obvious, isn't it, they are planning to steal books from the collection. As unbelievable as that may be. Roger Limbert doesn't surprise me for a minute, but Otto: incredible."

"This book you say you found in the encyclopedia, the something of gold. That's the one they're talking about on the tape?"

"Yes, it is. And the 'Roth' they mention is Theodore Roth, one of the university's most distinguished professors. He was killed just last Christmas in a plane crash. This whole thing is becoming quite clear to me now, Detective. Roth was a compulsive book collector. He had an enormous library. His daughter is in the process of giving it to the university. He was a scientist and one of the things he collected was work by Robert Boyle."

"Who's this Boyle?"

"Robert Boyle. A seventeenth-century scientist."

"So he's got nothing to do with all this?"

"Hardly. But one of the rarest of the Boyle books is this little tract on transmutation. Fulton's bibliography of Boyle claims there are only four copies known. As much as I hate to think so, it appears Vandersteen was willing to steal it from the Karlsson collection and sell it to Roth. Apparently with Roger Limbert as the middle man."

"So how did you end up with it?" Nielsen said.

"Well, I told you. It was in the box with the encyclopedia I bought from Alice Lowell."

"And why would that be? Why wasn't it sold to Roth?"

"I have no idea. Perhaps because he was killed in the plane crash, before Otto and Roger had a chance to settle."

"Nick, you said Alice Lowell bought the two boxes of books from Professor Stubblefield, who's the boyfriend of the dead guy."

"Right."

"And you know this how?"

Nick hesitated. "Well, I happen to know Alice's sister, Claire. She told me."

Nielsen studied him until Nick said, "Claire's an old friend of mine, from when she lived here in town. I told you that before. Your people have talked to her. She's just back from California."

"And?" Nielsen was mutilating another paperclip.

Nick laughed. "And she showed up at Gino's last night instead of Limbert. That's when she mentioned the books."

"She knows Limbert?"

"From California. They were friends there."

"Well, well." Nielsen leaned to the desk and wrote on the clipboard. His swivel chair squawked. He lifted the palms of his hands toward Nick. "Keep going."

"I might as well tell you this," Nick said, "but you'd have to know Claire to not take it too seriously. She was afraid Limbert wanted to talk to me because she thought he was going to blame her for Alice's murder. So she claimed it was Limbert who did it."

"That so. Why would she kill her sister?"

"Money. Whatever she would inherit, being the only relative. Apparently she's broke. She wants to go to New York and work in the theater."

"What'd she say about Limbert then? Why she thought he did it."

"She had this crazy idea that Limbert figured they'd get together again, after she inherited from Alice. Which is just nuts, really."

"Well, maybe they're in it together. And now the thieves have fallen out. That sort of thing. One's blaming the other."

"No way," Nick said. "You don't know Claire."

"You don't either," Nielsen said. "California changes people."

Sam shifted his big body in his chair. "I think you're chasing the wrong rabbit. It's the set of *Britannica* that's important. Obviously it was being used to store that tape you just played and probably other things. At least three of the volumes were hollowed out. Roger Limbert must have made that tape to hold over Vandersteen or maybe even Ted Roth. Probably he's a blackmailer. It wouldn't surprise me at all. Anyway, Stubblefield sold the encyclopedia to Alice without knowing what was in it, and Roger had to get it back. Apparently Roger wanted that tape, and whatever else he had in there, bad enough to strangle poor Alice."

"Why didn't he take the books, then?" Nielsen said.

"I don't imagine he wanted the books themselves. He took the tape, obviously. And maybe he was scared off. The store had just opened. Alice was lying there dead. Someone could have walked in while he was fooling with the books. There's another thing too. I was telling Nick this morning. Yesterday Roger made a point of running into my wife on campus—my wife is chair of the English department. He implied that he knew about some irregularity in Clarence Biedermann's travel expense account."

"The fellow that killed himself?"

"That's right. Clarence is—was—a professor in the department."

"What kind of irregularity?"

"Well, he never explained that. He was to see my wife today sometime about it."

Nielsen grabbed the edge of the desk and pulled his chair in again. He wrapped his arm around the clipboard as he wrote, as if to keep anyone from seeing it. "This Biedermann–he have a wife, or anything?"

"Yes, he had a wife. Pearl Biedermann."

Nielsen, writing, "What about Roth? Theodore Roth? He have a wife?"

"His wife is dead, but he has a daughter in town. June Roth. I believe she's living in the family house now, in College Heights. Actually, she was at the dinner at Stubblefield's the other night, too."

"That so. So she knew Limbert, then?

"Yes. She knew him."

"Who else was there, at this dinner?"

"Well, let's see: Biedermann and June Roth, my wife and I; Margaret Sawyer–she's Director of Libraries at the U. Otto Vandersteen was there; and Karlsson, the fellow who is giving the library to the U.; his daughter and her boyfriend. I believe that's all. The boyfriend worked in Alice Lowell's bookstore: Audie Thorson. Your police 'arrested' him along with me the other night, if you recall."

"I recall. Did anything happen? Like someone have a fight with Limbert. Anything like that?"

"At the dinner?" Sam said. "Not that I remember. Most of the conversation was about Karlsson giving the books to the library, and who was going to go out to the island to look at the collection. I was to go as the appraiser. Roger did make some comment about Biedermann's research trip. I don't recall just what it was. It made Clarence blush, as usual. And then–yes, he, Roger–also brought up something about could anyone steal books from the Rare Book Department. That got Vandersteen a little annoyed. Well that is interesting, isn't it? I see that in a different light now, given what the two of them were up to. He must have been baiting Otto."

Nick glanced at his watch and leaned forward, hands on knees. "I've got to get back to campus, Al. My dog's tied up outside, too."

Nielsen said, "First I wanna know what you make of this business between Limbert and your old girl friend. Mr. Ives here is making a pretty good case for Limbert being the one killed the bookstore woman. From the way you say they were blaming each other you gotta think maybe she was involved too."

"Roger Limbert never blamed her to me," Nick said. "Claire just thought he was going to. I don't know, Al. Like you say, I don't really know her anymore. I could maybe see her getting tied up in a blackmailing scheme with Limbert. She was always money hungry. But not murder. Especially her own sister."

"What about Limbert? Could she be the one that killed him?"

"I thought you said Stubblefield did that."

"Well, to tell the truth, we don't have a whole lot on the guy. Blood in his car. Like I say, he claims Limbert drove off in the car. The lawyer's gonna claim the killer brought it back and left it in the garage just to implicate the boyfriend. Which, I gotta admit, coulda happened. Professor Stubblefield will probably be out this morning yet. Soon as he gets a lawyer here."

"I don't see any reason for Claire to kill Limbert," Nick said.

"Thieves fall out. Like I say."

Nick stood. "Talk to her then. I told you all I know about it. I've got to get back to work. My dog's waiting out there."

"You bring that dog to work with you?" Nielsen asked.

Nick grinned. "Yup."

Sam stood, too, and brushed cigarette ashes that weren't there off his tie.

Nielsen said, "Mr. Ives, what I want from you is that other box of books. I'm sending an officer with you to get them. And what about that bit on the tape about finches? You know what that was about?"

"Yes," Sam said. "I was going to say. Nick said you found a list of bird plates along with the other volumes of the encyclopedia. I'm certain it refers to plates from the Audubon folios. Karlsson had a magnificent set in his library. I saw it yesterday. Apparently Vandersteen was quite willing to mutilate it—for money. Unbelievable."

"So the plate of finches he talks about is a picture of some birds?"

"Yes. I'm certain of that. Detective Nielsen, the boxes of books: I've paid for them, you know. They actually belong to me."

"I'm making a note of that."

"I'll get them back, then?"

"When this is over." Nielsen picked up the phone and pushed a button. "Is O'Brien out there yet? Tell him I need him." He got up from the desk and followed Nick and Sam to the door. "Mr. Ives, Officer O'Brien'll run you back to your place for those books. Nick, how 'bout you going with me to see this Vandersteen fellow?"

"What for?" Nick said. "Anyway, I've got the dog. I have to walk."

"Well, meet me there then, in front of the library. You know that place better'n me."

Nick smiled. "Libraries make him nervous," he said to Sam.

"Not true. I love to read books," Nielsen said.

ඥ

They left the elevator together, Nielsen walking slightly behind Nick, who led the way through the glass cubes of exhibit cases. Spotlights embedded in the ceiling were focused on the cases of displayed books, making them bright islands in the otherwise dim room.

"You never expect a place like this," Nielsen whispered to Nick's shoulder, "when you get out of that elevator. It feels like they slapped a museum on top of the rest of the place. Kinda an afterthought, like."

Mavis Martin greeted them at the reception counter.

"Is Mr. Vandersteen in, Mavis?" Nick asked.

She glanced toward the office suite behind a glass wall. "He is. At least I didn't see him go past here again. Check his office. Is something wrong? He looked kinda weird when he came in before." She whispered alongside her hand, "More than usual, anyways."

"We just need to talk to him, is all," Nick said.

"You want I should show you?" Mavis started toward the counter's swinging gate. "Maybe I should show you."

"It's okay, Mavis," Nick said over his shoulder. He was already pushing open the glass door to the offices and department workrooms.

Otto Vandersteen sat stiffly behind his enormous desk in a green leather chair that surrounded him like a throne. The orchid in its jardiniere on the desk's corner bowed its arc of yellow blossoms toward him. The fluorescent ceiling lights had been turned off but a metal floor lamp on a long stem leaned a silver shade over Vandersteen's shoulder. His face was pale, and pink patches splashed the top of his bald head like intermittent blushes. He looked like he was trying, by not speaking or moving, to contain a bad hangover, to prevent his glass body from being shattered by a sound.

"Mr. Vandersteen," Nielsen said in the doorway. "Detective Nielsen, city police. We met last year."

Vandersteen cautiously cleared his throat. "I remember."

"This here is Nick Ash, from campus police."

Vandersteen nodded. "Yes."

He didn't invite them in, so Nielsen crossed to the two chairs in front of the desk and pulled both out, but stood in front of them and did not sit down. Nick stood next to him with his arms folded.

Vandersteen shaded his eyes with one hand, as if against a glare. "Please sit down," he said. "I'm not feeling well this morning, gentlemen. I was about to go home."

Nielsen looked at the low chairs behind him and stayed standing. "You know a Roger Limbert, I understand," he said.

"Well I do, yes." His tongue quickly wet thin lips. His throat rattled, as if to clear a path for the next words. "I've only just learned of his death. It's shocking. I had dinner there the night before last. I know Professor Stubblefield quite well, more so than Roger Limbert. I just hope ... Would you both please sit down. I do not like to be looked down on."

The two men pulled up the chairs and sat forward on the edge.

"You hope what?" Nielsen asked.

"Well, shot like that, in the park, late in the evening. I just hope it wasn't a sex thing. It will be hard enough as it is for Alfred, I'm sure. He was quite upset with Roger already about some woman Roger was seeing."

"Woman?" Nielsen said. "Who would that be?"

"I've no idea. Roger had been seen ... Well, I just hope Alfred wouldn't have ... He was very distraught about it."

"Where were you last night, Mr. Vandersteen, around ten?"

Vandersteen's pale face seemed to shrivel. "Where was I? Why ... why ... why I was home. At ten I was at home. I dropped Stubblefield off at his house—we'd been to the Peninsula to inspect a library—I dropped him off about seven and I went home. Why do you ask? Surely ..."

"Anybody at home? Your wife? Anybody?"

"My wife was there, of course."

"Mr. Vandersteen. We have this tape ..."

"Tape?" The word quavered.

"A tape of a phone conversation between you and Roger Limbert."

Vandersteen leaned to the desk and put his forehead down on the polished surface. Nick and Nielsen stared at the shifting pink patches on his bald head. The narrow shoulders in the dark brown suit shook slightly.

"Mr. Vandersteen?" Nielsen said. He looked at Nick and shrugged.

Nick said, "Are you alright, Mr. Vandersteen?"

He raised his body slowly to sit upright in his chair again, his aging face like cracked eggshell, his eyes watery and large behind glasses knocked askew by the desk surface. He adjusted his glasses and in his throat made a sound that might have been an attempt to speak.

Nielsen said again, "We have this tape ..."

Vandersteen interrupted him. "Yes." He sighed. He reached to an ink pen on his desk and changed its position slightly. "I was afraid, when you came in here, that you might. I gave him quite a lot of money for it and yet he never gave me the tape."

"Who are we talking about here?" Nielsen asked.

Vandersteen stood and turned to the large window that looked out across rooftops and treetops and the top floor of a parking ramp. He rested an arm on the back of his chair. "Roger Limbert." He turned back to them. "Last night." He sat down again carefully. "When I got home last evening my wife said he'd called several times, insisting I call him. I did and he said it was urgent I meet him. I did and ..."

"Where was this? That you met him?" Nielsen asked.

"He came in Alfred Stubblefield's car, that laughable Buick. I went out and we talked in the car in front of the house. He said he was leaving town and needed money. He played the tape in the car's cassette player. Well, you know what's on it. I think it's only too clear what the situation was.

He said he would give it to the Director of Libraries. Or he could give it to me and leave town for good. We drove to an ATM–the one on the corner of University and Park–and I withdrew a thousand dollars from my account, all that was allowed. He said he needed more. We argued. I had money in the house from something I had recently sold. We went back there and I gave him another two thousand. Then he said he'd mail me the tape, after he got out of town, so I wouldn't go to the police. What could I do? Then he drove off."

Vandersteen picked up the ink pen and began to turn it with two fingers end over end. A small smile tipped the corners of his mouth. "At least it should show that I didn't kill him. I wouldn't have given him all that money first. And I would have the tape."

Nielsen said, "There was no money found on him."

"You can quite easily check the bank records, detective. You'll see the withdrawal."

"Yeah, well maybe you did give the money to him and then you took it back after ..."

Vandersteen popped to his feet. "I did not kill Roger Limbert." His voice was about to break into a sob. "You ought to be talking to Alfred Stubblefield. They were having a terrible fight. Alfred was almost afraid to go into the house when I dropped him off last night."

"Yeah, we thought we might do that," Nielsen said. "I think you'd better come with me, Mr. Vandersteen. We'll need a statement from you down at the station."

"Yes," Vandersteen said, dazed. He looked around for the telephone, as if he didn't know where he had put it. "I should just call my wife."

"You can do that at the station," Nielsen said.

"Yes. Yes, I suppose." Otto Vandersteen started around his desk in his brown suit that seemed to have become suddenly so large for him that he appeared to be moving inside of it. Then he fainted, and his bald head bounced once on the sound-absorbing carpet.

℃

June Roth's right cheek was pressed into a small puddle of drool on the surface of her father's desk, her slightly opened mouth pursed as if set to whistle. And a tiny whistle did sound behind her teeth as she breathed. On the desk her white arms circled her head like a halo. A patch of blood on her right forearm had dried enough to begin to flake off, and the shoulder of her blouse was stained with crusted blood.

The birds woke her: finches flying in a flock from their opened cages in the kitchen just at the moment the morning sunshine was about to break through the two windows behind the breakfast table. They passed through the dim living room and into the library to alight on chair backs and the edges of lampshades, chirping. Two fluttered down toward the sleeping woman, but at a sudden grunting snore they averted and rose to cling with tiny orange claws to the warp of the drapes. More than the soft sound of miniature wings, and chirps no louder than a mouse squeak, was needed to wake June Roth from her exhausted sleep. The bravest bird dove from a curtain rod to the top edges of the books on the desk and from there hopped into the nest of June Roth's hair. She awoke with a start, lifting at first only her wide-eyed head, dazed, seeing only the paraphernalia of the desktop. The bird flew out of her hair.

"Timmy?" she said, looking up.

Her father's portrait watched her from above the fireplace. She began to remember last night. She brushed at the dried blood on her arm and on the shoulder of her blouse. Everything blurred behind the sudden welling of water in her eyes.

"It was all a lie," she said aloud. She rubbed her eyes with the back of her hands. "No one would ever believe a word of it." She was speaking now to her father.

She remembered the tape then and pulled open the desk drawer. The tape cassette lay among paper clips and dried rubber bands. She lifted it out with two fingertips, as if the black tape coiled inside were some kind of poisonous snake prepared to strike.

"And no one will ever hear a word of it," she said aloud and dropped it on the desk, already in her mind burying it in the backyard.

The birds came to land with a little forward tilt on her shoulders and her arms and to hop about the desktop, but June Roth, ignoring them, sat very still and straight in her chair and stared at the tape cassette and remembered last night.

By eleven o'clock she had decided the woman wasn't going to come after all, that it was someone's filthy practical joke. She had been convinced it was either Stubblefield or Roger Limbert who had called earlier, who had written the note to slander her father. But neither one had come in the hour the caller had said, and the second call had come from a woman. What woman would know anything about her father's rare books or the Audubon print he had brought back from a trip as a present for her birthday? Then she thought of Margaret Sawyer and her face flushed red. Margaret Sawyer. And she remembered that only last fall her father had mentioned to her rumors about Friends of the Library funds that had gone missing, funds that had been in the safe in the Director's suite, a safe to which only Margaret and her secretary knew the combination. For weeks gossip had swarmed like bees among the librarians, but nothing had ever been proved. Margaret Sawyer. She tried to remember what Margaret Sawyer had said to her at Stubblefield's dinner party. Had they even talked?

The car had come at eleven thirty. June had been wandering the study floor, walking the perimeter of the Oriental rug and talking loudly to the alarmed birds. She saw the headlights flash like lightning across the drapes as the car pulled into the driveway. She waited. Her heart began to pound. But she heard no car door slam. She peeked around the lace curtain on the side window overlooking the driveway. The car had stopped there, its headlights on. It had been raining and the wet car gleamed with light reflected from the house. She went quickly through the living room and the kitchen and out the back door. She walked in the glare of the headlights toward the idling car. She stopped and stared at the enormous, brilliant eyes as would a dazed deer. Night insects rose from the wet grass and swarmed into the light: mayflies and mosquitoes and a moth as big as a sparrow whose bumping and fluttering against the headlight broke the spell. She passed out of the light and around the side of the car to the already opened window. She leaned in, shading her eyes blinded by the black after-images of light, and before she could speak a woman's voice said, "Get in."

"Margaret?" June Roth said.

"Get in the car," the voice said.

She opened the broad door of the old Buick and slid onto the seat.

"Shut the door," the woman said.

June could see the dark shape now, dimly lit by the lights of the dashboard: blond hair, a sleeveless red dress, a pretty face she did not know. She felt something wet against her arm and she pulled away from the doorframe. "Who are you?" she said. "What is this all about?"

The woman had turned to look over her bare shoulder as she backed the car out of the driveway.

"Where are you going?" June demanded. "Let me out of this car." She realized now that she had forgotten her purse with the gun.

The backing car bumped across the dip of the gutter and turned into the street. "Just shut up and listen to this," the woman said. She punched something on the row of lighted buttons on the dashboard. The tape hissed for over a minute before a voice that June recognized immediately, in spite of the scratchiness, began to speak. She felt the blood rush away from all her skin into a thudding core under her breast. She covered her mouth with a hand of ice.

"*I can't talk to you here,*" her father said. "*I'm in a meeting. Do you have the list?*"

"*How long? The meeting?*"

"*I'll meet you at one on the Union terrace. But I'm leaving for San Francisco this evening, so I won't have much time.*"

"*He copied down the titles of all of the books by Boyle that were there.*"

"*Who did?*"

"*Vandersteen. What'll you pay for the whole lot, if we can get them out of there?*"

"*I don't want all of them. I told you I already have several in my own collection. Was* Degradation of Gold *there?*"

"*Let's see. Yeah, it's on the list.*"

"*Yes. I was certain he was the one who bought it.*"

"*What'll you pay for it?*"

"*We'll discuss that. It's the only one I really want. In fact, I think it's best to take only that one. I don't think you should risk someone noticing books are missing.*"

"*Who's going to notice? Karlsson doesn't know beans about the collection, according to Otto. And Otto's the one who'll take care of processing it when it comes to the library.*"

"*Be that as it may, I only want the* Degradation.*"

"*What about the Audubon plates, like the plate of finches you gave your daughter? You want anymore?*"

"*No. I just wanted the finch plate. She's very fond of finches, and it was for her birthday.*"

"*If you want anymore, it would only cost you two thousand a plate.*"

"*No. I feel guilty enough as it is. I've always been against mutilating books for their plates, as so many book sellers do.*"

"*I looked up the turkey. That's worth ten thousand alone.*"

The voices stopped and June Roth, hand over mouth yet, stared at an amber light glowing on the radio. The car moved slowly under the old trees dripping spent raindrops onto the streets of College Heights.

"You get what that was about?" the woman asked. She drove with both hands on the top curve of the steering wheel. "In case you don't, your father was stealing books. Or at least he was buying stolen books that he asked somebody else to steal for him. Now, I've been told your father was a pretty big deal at the university—Nobel Prize and all that—so I'm sure you wouldn't want anybody else to hear that tape, for the sake of his reputation, and all."

June could feel the woman looking at her now, but she kept her eyes on the wet blacktop flooded with light from the car's headlights.

"Now, this whole thing isn't going according to how I planned," the woman said, "so you're getting a break. We're going to drive to an ATM and you're going to get all the money you can out of it, and then I'll give you this tape. Then I'm out of town and you'll never hear from me again. Okay?"

June turned to look at her then. The woman's hair was messed and looked wet. She was frowning as though she had a bad headache.

"Who are you?" June said.

"Never mind that. What kind of money can you get?"

Something wet on the seat back touched June's elbow and she jerked away. "I don't have much money," she said. She put her fingertips on her elbow and looked at her fingertips but it was too dark to see what had stained it.

"Don't give me that," the woman said. "Your father had buckets of it and I know you're the only one left. There's an ATM on the corner of Park and University. You want this tape, don't you?"

June sighed and put her hand over her eyes. "This is all a lie. My father ..."

"What's your number? The pin number?"

"You'll have to go back to the house, then," June said. "I don't have my purse."

The woman stared at her. "Shit."

"Well, I don't have my purse. You'll have to go back to the house."

The woman slammed on the brakes and June flew forward and her shoulder hit the dashboard. The car skidded on the wet blacktop almost to the curb. The woman put her head down on the steering wheel.

"Shit," she said. "This is not going right."

June thought the woman was going to cry but she suddenly sat upright again and swung the car into a U-turn, accelerating so the car's rear fishtailed.

"Alright, so we'll go back," she said. "We'll go back." She hit the steering wheel with the heel of her hand.

In the driveway again, as June was getting out of the car, the woman said, "Just remember, you don't come back I'm sending this tape to ... to the proper authorities."

When June returned she sat on the passenger seat again but she did not close the car door. She kept her hand in the vinyl purse in her lap.

"You got it?" the woman said. "Shut the door."

"I don't think so," June said. She pulled out the little gun and pointed it at the woman. "Just give me the tape please."

The woman stared at the gun. "Gads," she said. "You old slut. Where'd you get a gun?"

"Just give me the tape. I may shoot you anyway. My father ..."

"Oh screw your father." The woman, furious, punched a button on the radio and the cassette door opened.

June reached for the tape, put it in her purse, and, keeping the gun aimed at the woman, got out of the car. She slammed the door as hard as she could.

"You old slut," the woman hollered through the closed window. She backed the car out of the driveway so fast the rear bumper scraped the road as the tires bounced over the curb. The tires spun on the wet blacktop as the car accelerated.

Still sitting at her father's desk, where she had slept all night with her head on the desktop, June Roth stared at the plastic cassette case. "It's all a lie," she said. One of the finches hopped across the desk and began to peck at the tape. With the side of her hand June slid the tape until it dropped into the opened desk drawer. She shut the drawer and stood. Her skirt felt stiff and she brushed at it. She scratched at the crust on her arm. It was then she realized she was covered with dried blood.

C8

Margaret Sawyer's office door was closed against the usual morning assault by her complaining staff. "I'm not in this morning," she had said to her secretary. "I have a report to finish." Egg-shaped in a loose blue blouse and blue slacks, she sat like a brooding Buddha in the jungle of her tropical plants. Her eyes felt to her like doll's eyes: plastic with a painted stare. She pulled off her glasses and threw them to slide across the desk until bumping against a precarious pile of papers in manila folders. She rubbed her eyes with both fists and a huge yawn broke out, distorting her plump face. How many times during the long night had she watched the illuminated numbers of her bedside clock click upward in their relentless count?

Well, she had told him off. These pipsqueak men give way like water when you challenge them. She had learned that long ago. She knew he could not possibly have any proof. And besides, everyone had benefited by the deal. The library most of all. Still, after the business with the Friend's money, it was best not to have any more gossip. She smiled slightly, thinking of the look on his face last night when she had risen as suddenly as a breaching whale from behind her desk and dragged him by an arm down the hallway, as if he were a child hauled to some dreaded punishment.

She almost leaped again from her chair in surprise as her office door burst open and a very large man whose shoulders all but touched each doorframe said loudly, "This damn place is worse than Chicago."

Margaret Sawyer leaned back in her chair with practiced nonchalance. "Mr. Karlsson. Was I expecting you?" She glanced at her wristwatch.

"I'll tell you what I wasn't expecting," Karlsson said.

"Please shut the door, Mr. Karlsson. Would you sit down, please?" Margaret rose from her chair as though she might be about to make him sit down.

"What is this, some kind of greenhouse," Karlsson said, looking around at all the plants. He grabbed the back of one of the two chairs arranged in front of the desk and pulled it further away to allow room for his long legs. "Smells like a swamp in here."

"What is it you want, Mr. Karlsson?"

"I come here, a woman gets strangled right across the street from me, a guy jumps off a cliff, and now they arrest your curator for shooting the guy who cooked supper for us the other night. This place is worse than Chicago. I'm thinking I'll take my daughter back home with me."

Margaret frowned. "Arrest? What are you talking about, Mr. Karlsson?"

"Otto up there. I was just there to see him and his secretary tells me the police just hauled him away, she thinks about the murder last night."

"Murder? Who was murdered?"

Over Karlsson's head Margaret saw her secretary waving at her in the doorway Karlsson had left open. "What is it Alan?" she said. She felt her heart beginning to pound.

"Mavis in Rare Books says she has to talk to you right away." The secretary held onto the doorframe as he leaned into the room, as if trying not to fall into something.

Margaret waved him away. "Excuse me," she said to Karlsson, and picked up the phone. "Yes?" she said, and listened for several minutes without interrupting. "Alright," she said. "I'll take care of it. Go about your work, Mavis."

"You didn't know about it?" Karlsson asked. "It was even on TV this morning. They found this Roger guy's body in the park last night. Someone shot him. This place is worse than Chicago."

Margaret stood and went to the fiddle fern obscuring almost half of a window. Habitually, she stuck her finger into the dirt and returned to her desk. She remained standing behind it, wondering if anyone had seen Roger Limbert here last night. Distracted, she said, "Was it something specific you wanted, Mr. Karlsson?"

"I'll tell you what I wanted. I'm calling this whole deal off, about the books. This whole process has been going on way too long, with all the red tape. Besides, I never realized what the old man's books are really worth till I talked with Ives yesterday. I'm making him a proposition; see if he'll sell the whole bunch on consignment for me. It'll be a good deal for him."

"Well that's disappointing, Mr. Karlsson. We had been planning for months now ..."

"That's just it—for months. I've got to get this moving."

As if from another room, Karlsson kept on talking while Margaret thought *I don't give a damn about the books, you idiot. Take your damn books. Could Roger Limbert have said anything to anyone about the computers? Probably not. Unless maybe Stubblefield.*

"Besides," Karlsson said, smiling, "you don't have a curator to take care of them anymore."

"Yes, well, I'll have to look into this, Mr. Karlsson. If that's all."

"You bet that's all." Karlsson marched to the doorway mumbling "Worse than Chicago."

Margaret Sawyer followed him and shut the door behind him. She crossed the room to the windows and peered through the shining foliage of her houseplants to the tarred rooftop of the bookstore across the library mall. Roger Limbert was dead. Vandersteen was arrested. An unaccustomed smile tried to raise the corners of her mouth. She could see no disadvantage in this to her.

CB

In his green leather chair, legs crossed, a cigarette burning itself out in the metal ashtray on the end table beside him, Sam Ives caressed with fingertips the paper cover of the little book he had kept hidden in the pocket of his white sport coat as the young cop lugged the box of encyclopedias from Sam's study and out of the apartment: Sam warning him "Carry it by the bottom; I don't want the bottom tearing out", and the cop grumbling "Damn heavy for books."

Walt Whitman looked at him accusingly from Alma's chair, then licked his paw and rubbed his nose.

"It's my book," Sam said to him. "I paid for it."

He loved this kind of heavy, gray paper binding: eighteenth century, usually Italian. Too bad it had gotten creased, but he could fix that. He held the little book up to his face, opened to the title page: *OF A DEGRADATION OF GOLD Made by an ANTI-ELIXIR: A STRANGE Chymical Narrative. LONDON, Printed by T.N. for Henry Herringman, at the Blew Anchor in the Lower Walk of the New Exchange, 1678.* With a tobacco-stained finger he traced the black type of the title on paper still crisp and white, smiling, feeling the thrill of knowledge.

Absorbed with the little book he forgot completely Alfred Stubblefield, Otto Vandersteen, Roger Limbert. He turned each page carefully. The margins had been cropped a bit, but not enough to touch the text. And the crease might affect the price a little. What could he sell it for? He knew the historical importance of the book in the conflict between Boyle and Newton over the new ideas of chemical elements and of the continuing fascination of both men with alchemy. From Fulton's bibliography of Boyle he knew there were only four copies yet in existence, three of them already in institutions. Ten thousand? Fifteen?

The cigarette hanging precariously in Sam's lips leaped when the phone on the end table rang, and cigarette ash fell into the crease of the book's inner margin. He jumped from his chair and blew and blew at the ash. Tiny veins on his cheeks turned red.

"Damn," he said, as Walt Whitman ran for the kitchen.

"Sam Ives," he said into phone. "Yes, Mr. Karlsson."

So an hour later, when Alma Ives entered their apartment, Sam was pacing the floor, hands gripped behind him.

"Good lord," she said, "is this what you do during the day? Pace the floor and fill the place with cigarette smoke. You could open a window, at least."

"You're early," Sam said.

She crossed the room to a window. "I just had to get out of there. The department's in complete turmoil, what with

Biedermann and now this business with Alfred. At least he's out of jail. The lawyer phoned. Sam, will you stop pacing. You look as if you're about to explode."

"Karlsson called," Sam blurted. "He wants me to sell his books for him. On consignment. The whole library." He grinned as if he had just won the lottery.

"Sell his library! What about the university? His gift?"

"He's upset. Says it's worse here than Chicago. He's taking his daughter and going home."

"How ridiculous. I hope you told him no. How could you possibly sell his library? From what Alfred's told me it would fill a warehouse. Honestly, Sam."

The apartment door burst open with Stubblefield still pounding on it. Walt Whitman, who, had curled up in Alma's chair, ran for the kitchen again.

"Alma, thank God," Stubblefield puffed. "I called the department and they told me you'd gone home already." He looked at his wristwatch as if to question why so early.

Alma and Sam were so startled they only stared. He looked like the homeless men they often encountered in the mornings on State Street or Fountain Square or the library mall: unshaven, his bloodshot eyes half hidden by swollen, tear-stained cheeks, his white hair a tangle. A wrinkled white shirt, close to being out of his pants, was bloused over his belt. He had taken off his pink tie and stuffed it partially into the breast pocket of his sport coat and it hung down the brown corduroy like the tongue of an exhausted dog. One hand was pressed tightly to his chest to slow a pounding heart.

"Good heavens, Alfred ..." Alma started to say as Stubblefield stumbled to her wing chair and collapsed into the enfolding arms of upholstery.

"I think I'm going to die," Stubblefield said with the deepest sigh he could manage.

"You look like you have already," Sam said.

"Sam," Alma warned. "Alfred, you should be home in bed."

"Of course I should," Stubblefield said. "That idiot lawyer you sent me wouldn't even give me a ride. And the police, well forget it. I *walked* here from the police station." He held his arms wide to display himself. "Like this."

"It's terrible, Alfred," Alma said. "We'll give you a ride home of course. Sam, you come with."

Stubblefield pulled himself up in the chair and, elbows on knees, put his face down into the palms of his hands. "Roger's dead, you know," he said through his fingers. "They think that *I* killed him."

"Well, that's nonsense, of course," Alma said.

"Not that I couldn't have." Stubblefield looked up at them. "I was angry enough."

"What happened, Alfred?"

"We had a terrible fight." He looked at Sam. "After I got back from our trip to the island. Otto dropped me off. You should see his new car, Alma. Really, I mean, for a librarian. Where does he get the money? I somehow felt there was going to be trouble with Roger. We hadn't been getting along well for the last few weeks. He was so nervous about something. Maybe not nervous so much as tense. Something. He wouldn't tell me. You must have noticed at dinner the other evening. I was sure everyone had noticed how nasty he was being. We'd had a fight just the day before, simply because I had sold some books to Alice Powell—my eleventh *Britannica*, which I simply did not have room for anymore. I had to make room for other things, so they just had to go. Along with various paperbacks, etcetera. Well Roger, it seems—without telling me, of course—had stored some letters or papers, whatever, in them, and he was absolutely furious at me. Alice had come over in the evening to pick the books up and Roger was out again, of course—like he has been so often lately.

Alma said, "Sam, it must be the encyclopedia you bought from Alice. Did you know it was Alfred's?"

"*You* bought it?" Stubblefield said. "It wasn't really in very good condition, Sam. I'm surprised. I hope you didn't pay a lot. Well, I'm glad to know. Did you find Roger's papers? He'll be glad to ..." He covered his face with both hands.

"Alfred, dear," Alma said. "I think you should let us take you home now."

He looked up and rubbed an eye with the heel of his hand. "I forgot," he said. "For a minute. About Roger. It's really so unbelievable."

Sam said, "So Roger was furious, you said, about selling the books. What'd he do?"

"Do? Well, it was too late when he got home that night to do anything. I told him I'd talk to Alice in the morning. I did try. Remember, Alma? We were walking in to campus together and I stopped at the shop but she wasn't open yet. After that it was too late, of course. After one of those creepy street people murdered her. And for what? A few dollars at most. Poor Alice."

"So you had another fight last night, you and Roger?" Sam said. "About the books again?"

Stubblefield noticed the tie hanging out of his pocket and stuffed it in out of sight. "Not about the books," he said. He inspected the backs of hands. "He was in a terrible mood. I should have known enough to let it be, but Otto had just told me he'd seen Roger with some woman–on the Union terrace, more than once, too–and I simply asked him who she was. Well, you'd think I'd accused him of murder, the way he exploded. Said he'd had enough of my ... Well, what's the point in ... He said he was going away. Nothing was working out for him here. He said very cruel things to me and then he stormed out of the house." Stubblefield turned his face, drooping with sadness, to the apartment door to demonstrate the devastating departure of Roger. "And that's the last I saw him."

"He took your car then?" Sam said. "He was going to leave with your car?"

"Well, he wasn't going that very instant. I assumed he'd come back for his things. He was just being melodramatic, storming out like that."

"But only your car came back, covered with blood."

"Sam!" Alma scolded. "That's enough now. Come, Alfred, we're taking you home."

Stubblefield tried pushing himself out of the chair with as much effort as possible. "Your husband is worse than the police, Alma," he said, falling back. "They think I killed him, you know: Roger." He looked over his shoulder. "Do you suppose ... I would really like a drink about now, Sam."

"Good idea," Sam said. He ground his cigarette out in the ashtray and got up. "Alma?"

"Not now," Alma said.

"Just a small bourbon," Stubblefield called to Sam at the liquor cabinet. "One ice."

"Here you are, Alfred." Sam handed him a cut-glass tumbler and dropped back into his chair, holding his own drink up to keep from spilling. "That *Bleak House* of yours."

"There's no ice in here," Stubblefield said, peering into the glass.

"We don't have ice."

"Don't be ridiculous, Sam," Alma said. "Give it to me, Alfred." She took his glass and went into the kitchen.

"That *Bleak House* of yours," Sam repeated. "Where'd you get it?"

"Get it? I bought it."

"Yeah? From who?"

"From whom."

"From whom did you buy it?"

"I told you the other night. I'm not telling that."

"I don't think you bought it at all, Alfred. It came from Karlsson's collection, didn't it."

Stubblefield's face immediately turned pink. He pressed one had to his forehead.

"The box the parts are in," Sam said, "is the same as the ones on all the other Dickens in Karlsson's collection–same crimson leather label even–and I noticed when we were there Karlsson didn't have a *Bleak House* in his collection. I checked specifically."

"I didn't steal it," Stubblefield said. "I paid dearly for it. Too much, I'm sure. If you must know, I bought it from Otto Vandersteen, just last week. He was selling some of the rare book duplicates, for the benefit of the Friends of the Library. I knew I was paying too much, but, you know, as long as it was for a good cause."

"And it just happened to have the same box as those in Karlsson's collection."

"Sam, you pointed that out when we were at Karlsson's. I told you it's a perfectly generic box. There's nothing distinctive about it."

"Except the crimson leather label. I know how much those cost. It's something a collector would order specifically. And it was obvious a bookplate had been removed."

Alma returned with Stubblefield's glass. He reached to take it with trembling hand, clinking the ice cube. He swallowed half and winced. "Why do you plague me with this now?" he croaked, holding his double chin. He put the glass on the end table and stood. "If you're so interested in that silly box ask Otto. I really have to go now." He tucked in his shirt and brushed at the front of his wrinkled pants. "Can you drive me, Alma?"

"Of course," Alma said. "Sam, you come too."

Sam grunted and pushed out of his chair. "It'll be rush hour traffic, you know." He retrieved Stubblefield's glass from the oak end table he treasured, and with his handkerchief soaked up the rim of water the glass had left.

"I dread going back to the house," Stubblefield said. "And what will I ever do with the car? I'm certain I will never enter it again."

"Who do you think killed him, Al?" Sam said as the three of them moved to the door.

"Sam," Alma warned.

"Just wondering," Sam said. "Thought he might have some idea."

"Well I don't," Stubblefield said. "And how the police could have thought I had done such a thing is beyond me."

"Funny the blood was all on the passenger side," Sam said.

"Sam, that's enough," Alma said. "Alfred doesn't need to talk about this now."

Stubblefield had stopped in the doorway. He looked at Sam in surprise. "It was? The police didn't say that."

Sam put his hand on Stubblefield's shoulder. "Somebody else besides Roger was driving your car last night, old boy."

# TEN

After leaving Nielsen and the ambulance that had taken away the weeping Otto Vandersteen, Nick checked in at Protection and Security.

"Some woman's been calling for you all morning," Rose Delaney said. She reached to retrieve a notepad from next to the telephone on her desk. "A Clarisse Lowell. What's going on, Nick? Why the ambulance call at the library?"

"Just somebody passed out, is all," Nick said. He didn't want to explain everything to her yet. "She didn't leave a number?" He balled up the note Rose Delaney had handed him and threw it toward the wastebasket.

Rose leaned back in her chair and put her hands behind her head. Nick noticed the rise of her breasts under the khaki uniform shirt. "No, she didn't. Who's this Clarisse? She seemed pretty excited about something."

Belle walked around the desk and put her nose up to Rose to be scratched.

"Hello there, dog," Rose said. "How'd it go with the dog today?"

"Fine," Nick said. "No problems. Can I just grab your phone book there? I need the number."

Rose watched him flipping the pages. "She has to catch a plane, she said. Old girlfriend?" She pushed the notepad across her desk to Nick and he picked out a ballpoint from a mug and bent over the desk to write the number.

Nick looked at his wristwatch. "I might have to take the afternoon off," he said. "Okay? I've got vacation time."

The way Rose Delaney looked at him he knew she was thinking of the many days he hadn't shown up at all, or even called in, sheets and blankets pulled up over his head in broad daylight to make the world as dark as his soul.

"Alright," she said, dragging out the word to make sure he knew she didn't want to say it. "Just so somebody's covering lower campus."

He decided he didn't want to talk to Claire on the phone. He took the dog back to his apartment first. He thought of getting his bike down off the back porch, but he knew Claire would think he looked ridiculous riding a bike—the Hollywood girl; she used to laugh at him about it even when she lived here. So he walked the two miles down Regent Street. Most of the old elms had died long ago, so the afternoon sun was hot. He felt a line of sweat slide down his spine under the khaki shirt of his uniform.

Alice Lowell's house stood in a cluster of small, wood-frame houses at the edge of College Heights. Close together, only a narrow driveway separating them, they were hidden from the curving streets and elegant homes on the hill by a canopy of oak trees. In window boxes under the shutter-framed windows of the house, shade tolerant plants (impatiens, begonias) hung limp from lack of water. The grass was uncut. Crab grass clutched the edges of the walkway to the house, and dandelions grew in cracks between the concrete slabs. Nick was still halfway up the walk when Claire pulled open the door and stood holding the screen door open.

"Jeez, finally," she said. "I've been trying to get you forever."

She was wearing a yellow summer dress cut square across her breasts with white straps over her tanned shoulders. When he tried to brush by her while she held the door for him, she turned to him and he almost had to hold her.

She smelled of soap and hair spray and cigarettes and too much perfume. He put his palms up toward her as if to put a pane of glass between them and moved into the hallway. Two large suitcases draped by a white plastic clothes bag stood at the bottom of a stairway.

"Leaving town?" Nick asked.

"I told you I was. Last night. I just wanted to say goodbye, is why I called you." She looked at her wristwatch. "I don't have much time, either. Come on in the living room, Nicki."

She turned through the arched entry into a room cluttered with old upholstered furniture arranged around the perimeter of a round braided rug. A grand piano was squeezed between a row of windows and the back of a sofa. Precarious towers of books and piles of sheet music covered the top of the piano and more books were stacked on top of the sofa's back, where it met the side of the piano. Some of the books had fallen onto the cushions below. Two walls were lined with bookcases crammed with books, and books were piled on the hardwood floor at the foot of the bookcases. A dusty Christmas cactus in a jardiniere was dying on its plant stand.

"Can you believe this place?" Claire said. "I can hardly wait to get out of here. I just hate books. Don't sit on the sofa, Nicki. It's covered in dog hair. That stupid dog. Sit there, that chair."

"I don't want to sit, Claire," Nick said. "Where are you going?"

"I told you. New York." She looked at her watch again. "I've got a flight."

"So what did you want me for?"

She smiled at him, head to one side, looking up in her old teasing way. "I want you to come with."

"Come on, Claire. You know I won't. What do you want?"

"A favor, then."

"What favor?"

"I saw a lawyer, like you told me, Nicki, but it takes like a long time to get an estate settled he said, and I've got these plans I told you about, so I was hoping you'd do that for me, Nicki, deal with the lawyer for me and see about selling the house and the store and all that and send me the money. His name is Tomchick or Tomchuck, Tom something. He's in the phone book. I signed all the papers he said to make you represent me. I'd really appreciate it, Nicki, if you could do that for me. And I'll let you know where I'm staying as soon as I find out. And the other thing is Alice. They wouldn't let me bury her yet–the police. So I was wondering if you could do that for me, too, when they say it's okay to go ahead. I hate to ask you all this, Nicki, but I really have to go to New York. I've got this audition, like in two days, and I don't know where I'll even be staying yet."

She moved from behind one upholstered chair to another while she talked. "It's kind of scary: New York, you know. I've never even been there before." She smiled at him. "I sure wish you'd go with me, Nicki."

"You're something else, Claire," Nick said. "What about your friend Roger?"

"Roger? What about him. He's not going with. He's with his gay friend now. Anyways, he's half the reason I'm getting out of here. I told you how scared I was of him. He's crazy, that Roger: going around hinting I could've killed my own sister."

"One of you did," Nick said. "Which one?"

"Nicki! How can you say something like that?"

She came from behind the chair toward him and he saw in her face anger and anxiety before she stopped halfway and hugged herself and changed her expression to what she must have thought was honesty. To Nick her face had suddenly become as plastic as her sprayed hair.

"It was Roger," she said. She dropped into the big armchair behind her, as though exhausted at the effort to be truthful, arms still crossed tightly over her breasts, legs crossed, the yellow dress above her knee. "Last night, after you left the bar, he showed up after all, acting all surprised you weren't still there waiting for him. I said to him 'You're just mad you don't have a chance to bad mouth me to him, is all, saying I would kill my own sister.' And he gives me this look he has, this scary look he's like Norman Bates or something, and he says 'I could kill you just as easy, you know, you don't do what I say.' That's what he said to me, Nick, 'I could kill you just as easy.' That's how I know he killed Alice. That's why I'm scared to death of him, Nick, why I'm getting out of this place."

"Why would he kill Alice?" Nick said.

"Why?" She crooked her fingers into her palm to look for a nail to chew, an old habit she had forced herself to break. She jerked her hand down and wiped the nails on her dress. She didn't look at him, and Nick could tell she was trying to think ahead.

"I told you last night," she said. "He wanted to get back those papers or whatever, that were in the books his friend sold Alice. He went to her store and she wouldn't give them to him and he said he had to have them so he killed her. He told me that, Nicki. Honest. And he would do that, too. Like nothing. You don't know Roger, Nick, what he's like."

"What was so important he would kill Alice to get?" Nick asked.

She frowned, thinking.

218

"Just tell me, Claire. No bull."

She stood and looked over her shoulder toward the kitchen. "You want a drink, Nicki? I could use a drink, if you want one. I get all nervous when I have to take a plane."

"No drink. Why'd he kill Alice, Claire?"

She looked at her wristwatch. "Jeez, Nick, I gotta go pretty quick. I should've called a cab already. What difference does it all make anyway? I just wanna get out of here, Nicki."

"What was so important he'd kill Alice for?" Nick repeated.

She sighed. "Alright, I'll tell you. But then I gotta go, Nick. I told you before Roger was not a very nice character, even though he befriended me in L.A. and I shouldn't say that about him. But, telling the truth, he had a way of digging up dirt about people and then he'd get money out of them about it, you know. Like blackmail. Anyways, he got in trouble with somebody too tough for him out there in L.A. and he came back here to get away. So one day he calls me and says I should come back home, too, he's working on ways to get a lot of money and we could go to New York together when he got it. So, things were not going so great for me in Hollywood, and all, and me being broke besides, I come back. And, telling the truth, even though I'm not proud of it, Nicki, I kinda missed the guy. Everybody thinks Roger is, like, gay, but believe me, I should know, Roger is not gay. At least not your average gay. Most of that gay stuff is a act of his. He always wanted to be an actor, but he was no good at it. Anyway, what was in those books his friend sold to Alice was some stuff he had on some famous professor here, for one thing, and another guy who was cheating on his expense account or something. Some other stuff, too, Roger was working on. Something about old books worth a lot of money. He'd spent a lot of time and effort getting this stuff together, so naturally he was pretty mad about it when Alice wouldn't give it back to him. I mean, Alice, really, if she'd known what Roger was like, she should've just given him the stuff and not argued."

"Why didn't you tell the police, if you knew he killed your sister?"

"I know I should have, Nicki. Poor Alice. But that's water under the damn now."

"You were in on the whole bit, right? The blackmailing?"

"I never did anything. Roger had it all going when I got here. I mean, I knew about it, sure. He told me about it. But I . never did anything."

"What happened last night, at the bar? You have a fight with him?"

"I was gonna leave right after you did, Nicki, but this fellow came over and said he'd like to buy me a drink, and ..."

"I don't care about that, Claire. What happened with Roger?"

"He came in all mad. All upset. Said everything was screwed up. He'd just had a fight with that professor he was living with–Stumblebum, or some goofy name–and the guy was going to turn him into the police, he thought. And besides that ..."

"Turn him in for what?" Nick said.

"I don't know, Nicki. Something about a book about Charles Dickens he said Roger had stolen. Which Roger probably did, knowing him. And besides that the one guy he was blackmailing had jumped off a cliff–if you can believe that–before Roger got the money. Roger could be such a screw-up. Jeez. Anyway, he just wanted to take off, and me go with him to New York. So I say, No way, what would we live on? No way without some money. So he says there's this woman yet, the daughter of the famous professor who got killed in a plane crash. He'd go see her and get money from her. He had these tapes, he said, she'd pay money for. So I said get going then, and that's the last I saw of him. So if I was you, Nicki, I'd call your police buddies and go arrest Roger for killing my sister, not to mention all the rest. And I'm calling a cab now or I'll miss my flight for sure. You're suppose to be there an hour ahead a time, like."

She sat in the chair again and picked up a dial phone on the end table and put it down again. "Shit. Where'd I put that damn phone book now, in this mess."

"Don't bother, Claire," Nick said. "You're not going anywhere yet."

She looked up and glared at him, her eyes squinted in hate. "Says who? You don't tell me what to do, Nick. You should remember that about me, at least. You don't tell me what to do."

"Did you kill Roger, Claire?"

"What're you talking about, kill Roger?"

Nick laughed. "I can see why you didn't make it in Hollywood. You're such a lousy actress."

"Very funny." She reached to a drawer in the end table, pulled it open, and dragged out a thick phone book. She began paging through it on the lap of her yellow dress. "Do they put it under 'taxi' or 'cab'?"

"They found his body in the park last night," Nick said.

"Roger's?"

"Knock it off, Claire. The police what to talk to you. I'm surprised they're not here already. Where's the gun?"

She couldn't resist looking at a green leather shoulder bag on the floor, leaning against the suitcases. She stood and stepped between Nick and the bag.

"If it's in there," Nick said, "that's all the police need, you know. It wasn't very smart to keep the gun, Claire."

She moved to him then and hugged him, pinning both his arms. He looked down into her plastic hair. She hugged him more tightly.

"Just come with me, Nick," she said into his chest. "Everything'll be great if you just come with me. Gads, you don't know all the problems I've had."

Nick pushed his arms out to break her hold on him. She started toward the leather bag but he grabbed her elbow and turned her back to him. "Just tell me about it, Claire. No lies."

"And then what? You'll arrest me?"

"I can't arrest you. I'm just a campus cop."

"So, you'll turn me over to your real cop buddies. You're such a sap, Nick. You never did know what's good for you. We could ..."

"There's no 'we,' Claire. Why'd you shoot Roger?"

She threw her chin up in anger. Nick knew that look: defiant, defensive; knew she would not be able to stop herself now.

"That little shit," she said. "You never saw such a screw-up. He gets me all the way back here with this big money scheme of his and then he wimps out. This one guy he's got on the string kills himself instead of paying anything, so Roger panics. Wants to quit the whole deal and get out of town. Last night, after you left, he comes into Gino's like I told you, all upset. He's gone and got money from the rare book guy, contrary to the whole way we'd planned it–got peanuts, is all, three thousand. He'd called the professor's daughter and was gonna meet her and get money, but first he goes to this library woman who he told me he's got proof she's been doing some crooked deals and she throws him out of her office. Can you believe it? The little shrimp. All this without saying a word to me. Then he comes into Gino's—he didn't even go see the professor's daughter, he's so shook up—and wants to quit. So I say, 'Okay, Roger, but first we'll go see the professor's daughter, since she's expecting you.' He's driving Stumblebum's car, so I say 'I'd better drive, Roger, you're so shook up,' and I drive him to the park, which I know from before has a reputation for being a drug hangout, thinking they'll blame it on some hop head, and I shoot him and leave him there, taking the three thousand bucks he did manage to get, of course. I thought maybe they might even get Stumblebum for killing him. I put the car back in his garage, with blood on the front seat, and all. Roger had left the door open. He'd driven me by there once to show off where he lived. So then I walked home from there."

She had been pacing back and forth in front of him as she talked, all the while looking at him. Nick knew she was gradually getting closer to her purse on the floor.

She said, "You don't even look surprised, Nicki. That nice girl you were so in love with once could shoot somebody."

"I don't get it," Nick said. "Why shoot the guy? You could've both taken off. The police weren't looking at Roger for anything. And why was Roger so anxious to talk to me?"

"I told you. He was going to tell you I killed Alice."

She threw the words at him like spit. Her fists were clenched.

"Why would he do that?" Nick said.

"Because I *did!*" she yelled. "I killed her because he was too chicken shit to do it. I went with him that morning to keep Alice distracted. Some guy was in there talking to her in the back of the store, so we had to wait behind some bookshelves until he left. Soon as Alice sees me she starts in, what did I want now. Roger starts arguing with her, he wants those books back. Not on your life, she screams. Get out. Both of you get out of my store. The dog leash was there on the desk. I picked it up and went behind her while she was hollering at Roger. It wasn't even that hard. I'm pretty strong, you know. And all the time that she was kicking and squawking and grabbing at the leash I just thought of how much I always hated her and her damn preaching at me growing up, acting like she was my mother or something. The worse thing was smelling her old-woman hair. My face was right in her dirty hair. But that just made me squeeze the harder. We found the boxes of books and got the tapes we needed. The whole thing scared the shit out of Roger. So later he decides to himself he's gonna take the three thousand he's got already and run, leave me holding the bag. Double crossing little shit. He was going to meet you at Gino's, get the cops on me for killing Alice, and take off. And there I am, instead of you, like he expected. He'd been dumb enough to tell me he had a 'date' with my old boyfriend. Roger always had to brag about how irresistible he was to guys. Knowing you, Nicki, I knew that was bullshit. Old Roger was up to something. So I show up at Gino's and he's late because he screws up with that library woman. The rest is like I told you. Roger starts to get panicky when I turn off to the park instead of driving him home. I drive down that path past the lion cages and down to the lagoon and old Roger is about to pee in his pants because I've got the gun on him now. He practically throws the money at me and says I can have it all and I should just get out, he'll never say anything. And he's right. Bang, bang."

"Geez, Claire," Nick said.

She smiled at him then, flirting again. "Come with me, Nicki. Please. The one thing is, you'll just have to learn to call me Clarisse, is all."

Through the window behind her Nick could see Nielsen getting out of the squad car.

# ELEVEN

Nick sat in the armchair facing Sam and Alma. He had told them all he knew. Walt Whitman sat upright on his lap staring at him. He wasn't purring.

"What's your problem, pal?" Nick said, rubbing the cat's ear between his thumb and finger.

"He wants your drink," Sam said.

"That's not it," Alma said. "He smells that dog on you. You've betrayed him, Nick."

Nick pushed the big cat to the floor. "Such is life, pal." He shook the almost-melted ice cubes in the bottom of his glass.

"You need another drink, Nick." Sam pushed with effort out of his leather chair.

"We're going down to eat soon, remember," Alma said.

Langdon Manor had a restaurant on the lower level where they often ate, since Alma no longer liked to cook. They had been about to leave for dinner when Nick had knocked on the door.

"Oh Nick, we're so glad," Alma had said. "Have dinner with us. We heard on the news about the arrest. Are you feeling awful? An old girlfriend."

"Get in here, Alma," Sam had said. "Nick needs a drink first."

The Scotch Sam handed Nick now was his second.

"Anyway," Sam said, dropping back into his chair, "I'm excited about it. Alma thinks I'm nuts, but I've got an idea."

"Talk sense to him, Nick," Alma said. "Do you see anywhere in this apartment he can put ten thousand books?"

"Here's what I'm thinking, Nick," Sam said. He leaned toward Nick, forearms on the knees of his white pants, the drink clutched in both hands. "What I'm thinking is Alice

Lowell's store is going to be for sale, once this mess is all cleared up. She always told me she owned the whole building, second floor apartments, too. I'll buy the place, clear out all the cheap stuff there, and use the Karlsson library as my base stock. It's worth a fortune, Nick, and the great thing is I can do it on consignment. No cash outlay. I'll fix up a nice office in the back to keep my mail order business going."

"Now you are crazy, Sam," Alma said. "Do you have any idea what a building like that would cost? We don't have that kind of money."

"Well, I'll rent it then, from whoever buys the building. I could even have a little area for antiques. Arts and crafts pottery and the like. Which I know a lot about."

"Valuable books and antiques in an old fire trap like that?" Alma said. "You might as well leave them out on the street."

"Come on, Sam," Nick said. "I don't see you sitting in a store all day."

"Won't have to. I already know who'll do the day to day running of the place. Make sure there's someone on the floor. Audie Thorson. He was already working for Alice. He's a bright kid and he needs a job. He told me so at Stubblefield's the other night."

"Audie?" Alma said, disbelieving. "He's a freshman."

"Maybe so, but he's older for a freshman. He was out of school a while. He's a very bright kid. I could tell, talking to him."

"Nick, tell him he's crazy."

"You're crazy, Sam." Nick took a deep drink of his Scotch and set the glass on a coaster. "I should get going."

"Oh no," Alma said. "You're having dinner with us. And we won't talk anymore about Sam's silly plans. I promise."

"The other thing I was thinking," Sam said, "is maybe I could get the university library to actually buy the whole collection, now that Karlsson's backed out on the gift idea. I'd get a nice commission that way, too. Too bad Vandersteen's out of the picture. I don't have much of an in with old Margaret Sawyer."

"Poor Otto," Alma said. "Will he go to jail?"

"He damn well should," Sam said. "Damn crook. How could someone charged with taking care of rare books cut plates out of an Audubon folio? Not to mention the books he stole from old Karlsson's library."

"He's in the hospital yet," Nick said. "His blood pressure went through the roof, I heard."

"What about June Roth?" Sam asked. "Has she heard the tape?"

"She has it. Claire told the police after they took her in that she had tried to get money out of June, too, with the tape. But June, if you can believe it, threatened her with a gun—her father's, I'd guess. One of the reasons Claire was so desperate to get away. Everything was going wrong for her too. Another thing, Sam. You're going to have to give up that little book you've got, the one on gold. It really belongs to Karlsson."

Sam sighed. "Damn. Well, it'll go back to the Karlsson collection and I'll get it that way. I was always going to sell it, anyway."

Alma stood and brushed at the lap of her lavender dress, either for wrinkles or cat hair. "Well at least Alfred should be relieved, not to be accused any longer of killing Roger. Although I'm sure he must be devastated, losing his friend."

"Some friend," Sam said. "That Dickens he's got, Nick—if I have to give back *The Degradation of Gold*, Stubblefield's got to give back that Dickens. He bought it from Otto and Otto stole it out of the Karlsson collection."

"Well, that's not my problem," Nick said. He had retrieved his drink but sat on the edge of his chair, as if intending to get up. The cat had returned to sit by his shoe and stare at him.

"You look so tired, Nick," Alma said. "You're feeling bad about the girl?"

Nick shrugged. "Not a bit. I hardly knew her anymore."

"Did she put up a big fuss, when the cops came?" Sam asked.

"They were such dunces, Roger and 'Clarisse.'" Nick tried to smile. "She even kept the gun. It was in her purse. I guess I just never figured she was that cold-blooded. But then, like I say, I really never knew her."

"Sam. I'm sure Nick doesn't want to discuss it anymore. Let's go to dinner now."

Nick stood and finished his drink. "Think I'll skip that, Alma. Thanks anyway. It's been a long day and I need to walk that dog yet."

"I knew it," Sam said. "He's going to use that dog as an excuse whenever he doesn't want to do something. 'Oh, I have to go home and walk the dog'. Why do people with dogs always do that?"

"Because they can," Alma said. "You would, too."

"Maybe we could use Walt for an excuse like that," Sam said. "Except, I suppose, cats can pee on their own."

"Well, thanks for the drink," Nick said. He started for the door.

"Will I see you tomorrow?" Sam asked. "On the terrace?"

"I'm not sure yet," Nick said. "I might take the day off. Go biking out to Fox Prairie."

"Thirty miles on a bike," Alma said. "You should stay home and rest up."

"Good night," Nick said.

When the door had closed, Alma said, "I'm worried about him, Sam. You know how bad he was after he broke up with that last girlfriend of his. Karen."

"He'll be alright," Sam said. "I think he's more embarrassed, than anything, that he could have cared for this woman once. Besides, I think he's getting interested in that female boss of his. Alma, tell me honestly what you think about my idea of a bookstore."

ος

On his way home, Nick walked along the lake path instead of going through campus. Across the calm lake the last rim of the sun had just slipped behind the line of trees and the light in the oaks he walked under began to fade to gray. Students passed him, walking or on bikes, heading for the student union or the library. A mother duck steered eight chicks in and out of weed-slimed rocks along the shore, feeding, and out on the lake a group of sailboats from the sailing club nodded on the smooth water. The young people on the boats were diving to swim since there was no wind to sail.

On the trunk of an old willow tree that leaned out almost parallel to the water, a boy and girl sat holding each other, their bare feet in the water, their backpacks sitting on either side of them like bookends. Then Nick felt the warm contentment from the Scotch inside him begin to fade as surely as the light in the trees and a blackness began to gather at the edges of his sight that he knew he had to fight against or he would fall down blind and trembling on the gravel path and strike out at anyone who tried to help him up again. That kid on the tree trunk doesn't know what he is in for. Be careful, kid. It can hurt so much. Two runners in shorts passed him and he began to jog after them and that felt better, so he started to run and he ran to the end of the lake path and past the crew house and he ran past the student dormitories and the tennis courts and the intramural fields where the games were ending and groups of boys were beginning to walk back toward their dorms. They looked over their shoulders at the old guy running in long pants and a long sleeve shirt. He cut across the soccer field toward the Ag campus and when he reached the greenhouses lined up like lighted ships in the beginning dark he stopped, heart pounding, chest heaving.

He walked the rest of the way home. Tomorrow he would get the bike cleaned up, everything adjusted, tires pumped, and ride out to Fox Prairie. That night for the first time he began to talk to his dog. He told his dog many things and his dog sat and listened to him and Nick felt a lot better.

# Author's Biography

John Neu served for forty years as Bibliographer for the History of Science in the University of Wisconsin Memorial Library in Madison, holding a joint appointment as Assistant Professor in the University's Department of the History of Science. After retirement in 2000, he moved to the Wisconsin north woods, near the small towns of Townsend and Lakewood, where he lives in a cottage on a lake. His previous novels include *The Tiger's Child* (2006), *Show Me the Way to go Home* (2009), *The Boy Detective* (2011), *The Dead Leaves Fall* (2012), *Dog Eat Dog* (2014), *The Dead of Winter* (2016), and *The Strange Things That Almost Happen* (2018).